SPANKY:
a soldier's son

S. L. LaNeve

My Climbing Tree, LLC
St. Petersburg, FL

This is a work of fiction. Names, characters, places and incidents are the product of the author's imagination or are used factiously. Any resemblance to actual persons, living or dead, events or locales is entirely coincidental.

Visit the author on the web at
www.myclimbingtree.com

ISBN 978-0983986515

To Don, who loves a good nickname,
gave me the creative space in which to flesh him out
and never let me give up. Thanks, Bun.
And to my mother, Audrey.
Thanks for being my champion.

CONTENTS

Part I

Part II

AUTHOR'S NOTES

ACKNOWLEDGEMENTS.

PART I

Chapter 1
Mouth-to-Mouth

When 'ole Blowfish found me mouth-to-mouth with my teacher, Miss Anders, I could've been a hero.

Me.

Spanky McDougal.

Hero.

Yep, that was me all right. This morning. Kneeling at her side. My whole class all crowded around us. And Jazz, oh man, Jazz. She finally noticed me. She kept yelling, "*Save her, Spanky! Save her!* I wasn't trying to be Superman or anything. No way. I just wanted to be like my dad. If he had seen me save Miss Anders, he'd have been so happy to have me for a son.

Only it didn't happen that way.

And I can't get Jazz's words out of my head.

"She's going to die, Spanky! I thought you knew what to do!

Chapter 2
Five Little Words

Clanging chairs give me a headache and my teeth will probably fall out from gritting them so hard. Kids are buzzing about whether Miss Anders will live. Some girl's crying. Counselors are supposed to show up so we can "talk about it." Only Jazz's words keep hitting me like machine gun bullets. *"Die, die, die. . . She's going to die, Spanky! I thought you knew what to do."*

A mug shot of me stares back from the cafeteria window. I blink a few times and the basketball courts come into focus. They're empty. After what happened this morning, part of me wants to run a bazillion laps around them. The rest of me is too tired to move an inch. And the sun is blinding me, demanding answers.

Explain why you froze McDougal. That would never happen to your dad. But then he's a real hero. Not a little weenie like you.

There's the huge oak tree next to the courts, the one I wanted to sit under someday with Jazz—like that's ever going to happen now. It reminds me of Dad. I squint and can almost see him leaning back against the trunk.

He's smiling up at me. I'm hanging from a limb and he roots me on. "That's two pull-ups, pal," he says, spooning out some of Mom's potato salad. "Let me see you do one more."

I don't want to erase that picture in my head. We'd only been in this stupid town a few days. DIP was having their annual David I. Patrick Back-to-School Family Picnic and Dad thought we should go. Mom wasn't so keen on it, not knowing anybody and all. But we went and picked a spot away from the crowd under that oak tree.

A crack of lightning scares my eyes open. When did it get so dark outside? Storm clouds are moving in, blocking the sun and drawing creepy shadows across my lap. The oak tree's branches are duke'n it out with the wind.

My eyes fill up and get all blurry again. I rub them with my sleeve real fast. Why does it feel like a zillion years have passed since that day with Dad?

It was only two months ago!

Talk about a dorky little kid. Back then, I'd been way too excited, wanting school to start. But that was before we'd moved. Before someone put my life on fast forward.

3

The summer had dragged like slugs crossing a sidewalk. Then Dad got laid off and bammo! We flash-packed all our belongings, crammed in Dad's truck and drove through the night, pulling a U-Haul behind us. Mom cried practically the whole way.

A little town in Florida called Appalacheeville was hiring firefighters. So that's where we were headed.

Another bolt of lightning flashes outside the cafeteria window, right behind that oak tree we'd all sat under. The hair on my arm stands up like it's saluting or something.

Oh man, that boom was so quick. Had to be close. And it's raining, again, like it's been doing every day for the last week.

A red truck with *Four Fat Guys and a Van* painted on the side pulls into the parking lot. And for real, four fat guys climb out wearing red coveralls. They're so big they kind of look like there's stuffing in their clothes!

For the first time all day, a chuckle leaks out of my mouth.

The four fat guys are unloading stacks of boxes and carrying them into the building, totally getting soaked. Reminds me of how my life got so messed up in the first place.

The packing and moving part hadn't been so bad when we left Pennsylvania. Changing schools where no one knew me actually felt pretty cool—kind of like drawing one of my sketches and erasing a few lines.

Only this sketch was me and I'd get the chance to redraw me all over again—just a little bit better.

But after we got to Florida, exactly one day before school started, I was in the kitchen, eating a bowl of cereal. Mom walked in, her eyes looking like a raccoon's with all that black smeary stuff around them, and started yelling at me.

"You aren't even unpacked yet. How am I supposed to count on you?"

I thought, count on me? And what made her so mad? I hadn't done anything.

Here's the thing. My mom has her bad days. Some really, really bad days. I knew not to make it worse. "Morning, Mom," was all I said.

I ate my cereal real quiet-like. Went back to my room and cleaned up my mess. Dumped clothes in my dresser drawers. Flipped the *Florida Snakes* calendar Dad had gotten me to the month of August—a coral snake—and hung it over my desk. Stacked my drawing pads and pencils on my nightstand. I did everything I could think of. I even vacuumed the floor to fix whatever I'd done to make her mad at me. Then I fell back on my bed and flipped open a sketch pad.

As soon as I saw the clean sheet of paper, I knew that going to a new school was going to be all right. Anything was possible.

I acted all stealthy that day after Mom yelled at me, waiting until my dad got home. "Under the radar," like he used to say. Maybe he'd know what had set her off. I even sketched the August coral snake for him. Its

5

different color rings reminded me of a jingle Dad used to tell me when we'd go camping.

If red touches yellow, you're a dead fellow.

If red touches black, he's a friend of Jack's.

We always kidded about finding Jack's friend. I was double-checking the order of the colors to make sure I had them right when the kitchen door bell Dad had hung jingled. I threw the pad on my desk and ran to the kitchen.

I swear all the guy had to do was walk in a room and the lights got brighter. Dad twisted me into a tight bear hug. "How's my number one son?" he asked.

"I can't breathe," I said, pulling away. I jabbed at his nose with my air gloves, stepping back, light on my feet. A left. Another left. A surprise right hook. Then I nodded in Mom's direction and shrugged.

Dad could usually cheer her up on one of her bad days. He swooped over to the kitchen sink, like a stealth bomber, and when he put his arms around Mom, she looked like a little kid.

Her hair reminded me of fire against Dad's dark beard. Didn't matter that he shaved every morning. By the end of the day his cheeks and chin seemed all smudgy from the hair growing back. He used to tease me that it was smoke and ashes from fighting fires.

Dad winked at me and called out, "Group hug!"

I didn't move right away. I mean, seriously, I was getting a little too old for group hugs. But it cheered Mom up, so when he waved me over, I mumbled, "Group hug," and let Dad pull me into their circle. I think that was the last time I felt so safe.

The hug was lasting way too long. Weirdly long. Getting uncomfortable long.

Finally, Dad pulled back. I expected him to start wrestling with me like he always did. Instead, he lifted my chin with his huge hand and didn't take it away.

He was smiling, which got me smiling. But he was also looking at me like he was challenging me to a staring contest. I stared back, trying to hold my eyeballs steady so they wouldn't blink, biting my cheeks so I wouldn't laugh. That's when I noticed those notches in the skin between his eyes that got deeper when something serious was bothering him.

"I've got some news for you, Spanky."

For a second, I got a little excited. He was going to say I could finally get the pet snake I'd been wanting for like a zillion years. The notches between his eyes were there because getting a snake was serious business. He had that same look the time he bought me a camping knife.

But that's not what he said. What he said was, "I got my orders today."

"Huh?" I repeated what he said in my head. *I-got-my-orders-today.* I couldn't believe it. I'd unpacked for nothing and we were moving a second time. "But we just got here!" I yanked my chin from his grip. "How can you get laid off again after only a week?"

Dad's smile disappeared. "It's not like that, pal. The Fire Department still wants me. But so does the

Army." He moved his hand to my shoulder. "Looks like the Reserves are sending me to the Middle East."

My legs got all wobbly like they might give way. "You're joking. Right?" I backed away. He had to be kidding. I smiled and said, "Yeah, right," bouncing my fists in front of my face to box with him again.

Mom started bawling into his chest. "No, Spanky. It's not a joke."

I stopped bouncing, my fists frozen in front of my face. My stomach cramped up. Way to go McDougal, I thought. Talk about a lame thing to say. So what if I was just a kid. I knew Dad was in the Reserves. I watched the news. The president was sending more troops overseas every day.

Dad pulled me back into their circle. The three of us stood there with our arms around each other, just breathing. Up close, Mom's skin looked red and blotchy and I guess she'd cried away all that black smeary stuff from the morning.

It was getting hard to breathe. I tugged on one of Dad's belt loops, but all I wanted to do was run—run far away—back to Pennsylvania if I could. "I'll be in my room," I said.

When I flipped on the switch, my bedroom light hurt my eyes. The walls were covered with a zillion little nail holes, probably from the last kid who'd lived here—holes and the coral snake, Mr. August, hanging over my desk.

I shuffled over and tore the sketch I'd drawn of him off my pad. I guess I went a little nuts, ripped it in half, crumpled it up and fired it at my wall.

My body felt all shaky. I fell into my desk chair. And as I stared at the blank computer screen, I got these pictures in my head, pictures of things I'd seen on TV. The desert. The sand-covered soldiers. The bombings. I tried to write D A D in the layer of dust on the monitor, but my hand shook so bad, it looked like my granddad's writing before he died.

It'd been a while since Dad and I had talked about those terrorist attacks that happened a long time ago. About how he couldn't just sit around and not do something to help. Saving lives was his job and all. He said one day the Reserves might need him. But why now? *I-got-my-orders-today.* I hated those five words.

"Hungry?" Dad was at my door, carrying a paper plate and smiling, like everything was okay. But I knew his smiles. This was his "things-are-messed-up-but-we're-going-to-make-the-best-of-it" smile. "It's my famous bologna sandwich," he said.

Sheesh. Everything Dad made was famous. His famous BBQ pork. His famous scrambled eggs. And his seriously famous homemade waffles.

My eyes filled up so I turned away real quick. "I'm not hungry," I said.

I felt his huge hand on my shoulder. "It's okay, pal. We can talk about this later."

When I looked up again, he was gone. The plate stared at me from my bed. I swear it whispered, "You

9

know you want me." I lunged for the sandwich and wolfed it down. Then I spun back around and the scribbly-looking D A D in the mess of dust on my monitor said it all. I was living in a strange house with bare, holey walls, school was starting, I had no friends, I was getting yelled at by *my* mom with her ups and downs, and now, Dad was leaving to fight some war in a desert.

Who would take me camping? Or help me at my new school? Who would box with me or tease me about being his number one son?

Who would cheer up Mom?

I got my orders. Five little words had totally messed up my life.

Chapter 3
Aimed Right Between My Eyes

The next morning was my first day of school and no coffee smells woke me up. No dishes clattered. No newscaster chattered on and on about traffic or the weather. The house felt way too quiet. And when I yelled for my mom, there was no answer. I threw on the shirt she'd ironed for me and headed to her room.

Boxes were everywhere. Talk about unfair! I thought how come she gets to yell at me about not unpacking? "Wake up, Mom! Did you forget what day it is?" I kicked an empty box aside with the toe of my sneaker.

"Oomph . . . I overslept." She rolled away from me. "It's just a temporary job, anyway."

"What? Mom, I meant school!"

She threw her spread off and rolled over. Then she pulled the covers back up and snugged them under her chin. "Oh honey. I'm sorry. Give me a second and I'll get up and fix your lunch."

I remembered the night before. How she'd cried most of the night. "It's okay," I said, and patted her foot through the covers. "I'll make it. Where's Dad?"

Mom closed her eyes again. "He had the early shift. You should go to school, Spanky. Try not to think about him leaving."

I'd been trying to do that. I might even have been able to. But as soon as she mentioned it, I lost that battle. "See ya this afternoon."

I left the house feeling kind of buzzy. Could have been the breakfast bar I'd wolfed down or maybe butterflies, it being the first day at a new school.

That ironed shirt I was wearing? Big mistake. Stepping out my front door was like walking into a steamy bathroom, but without a towel to wipe up the sweat. When I pushed forward, the muggy air pushed back. I wanted to rip off that shirt. I should have gone back and changed my clothes, but I was too excited and in too big a hurry.

At the bus stop, a baby green gecko with yellow spots skittered across the sidewalk. The little guy didn't even look both ways before he crossed. Didn't he know a huge foot might smush him into lizard paste? Probably excited about getting where he was going, too.

Stupid gecko.

I leaned up against a tree, thinking how wrong I'd been about this place. Before we'd moved, I'd seen this travel show on Florida. Sandy beaches and coconut palms. People holding drinks with little umbrellas

12

sticking out of them. Pretty girls in bikinis. When you live in Pennsylvania that sounds pretty darn good.

But Appalacheeville is too far north and smack in the middle of the state. So far, I haven't seen any girls in bikinis and the closest beach is more than an hour away. There aren't any palm trees, or at least the kind I was hoping for. Instead, we've got these ugly scrub pines. Their limbs look like twisted arms; the kind you see in scary movies.

That's when it hit me that maybe I'd been wrong about the bus stop too. Where were the other kids? Maybe I was standing on the wrong corner. What if the bus had already come and gone? I'd have to get Mom to drive me and it'd take me an hour just to get her up. I'd be late and have to interrupt the class and—

My heart was slamming so loud someone could've heard the banging coming out of my ears!

A bus pulled around the corner with the initials D.I.P. painted on the side. DIP. . . David I. Patrick School . . . had to be my ride.

I took a deep breath and made the quick decision to be friendly, but you know, not loser friendly. Like Dad always said, don't be showy; better to fly under the radar. If I looked a little mysterious, the kids might think I had more important things on my mind than being the new kid.

Which I did.

But I didn't want to think about it.

Up the steps, a girl in the front row smiled at me. Or not. She looked away so fast, I couldn't be sure. I scanned the seats around her, looking for an empty one.

The bus driver had other ideas. "New in town, sugar?"

Her sunglasses hid her eyes. All I could see was my reflection. A long gray braid stuck out of her University of Florida ball cap and her shirt was colored to look like gators were crawling all over it.

"Yes, ma'am," I said. My backpack slipped off my shoulder as I tried to edge by her.

"Slow down a second, son. I like to know all the kids on my bus." Gator lady closed the bus door and I swear her wrinkled arm was as big as my thigh. "I'm Alice Flagler, but the kids call me Miss Alice."

She smelled like suntan lotion and seemed to be waiting for me to say something. I whispered, "I'm Spanky, ma'am. Spanky McDougal."

"Well, now," she said, folding her huge arms in front of her. "I haven't heard that name in ages."

I moved my backpack around and held it close to my chest. "I get that all the time."

Miss Alice didn't move, didn't say anything back. Just stared and smiled. I wanted to tell her the truth. I hadn't gotten that in a long time. All the teachers and kids back home had called me Spanky since kindergarten. And if she thought Spanky was weird, well, she hadn't heard my real name.

But now, the kids up front were staring at me, too. And the edge of my snake book was pushing through the

14

been *humiliated* over being a Scout way too many times. They never had a clue about Scouting.

Not that I'm even sure anymore I still want to be one. Some of the stuff I heard. Whatever.

I leaned into him and cupped my hand over my mouth. "On my honor," I said, whispering the oath, "I will do my best, to do my duty..."

Skinny Kid flinched. Meanwhile, Army Guy was bending over to see what was on the floor.

My gut didn't trust the guy. I flung myself between him and the seat and grabbed the book. Only Army Guy was right there when I sat up and yanked it out of my hand.

"What'cha got there, new boy?" He talked with a serious southern twang. Maybe being a cracker had something to do with that.

Army Guy raised Skinny Kid's handbook and said, "Hey y'all," in a voice loud enough for kids around us to hear, but not for Alice to. "Look what the new kid's trying to hide."

A short, scrawny-looking guy sitting next to him was trying to take it from him. "Mack. Let me see it," he yelled, and then he snapped out three quick sneezes, the kind that barely makes any noise. "I can't weach it." Sounded like the guy had a speech problem.

"Boy Scouts of America," said Army Guy, a.k.a. Mack, slouching in his seat. "A Handbook for Boys. And it's this new kid's. Now isn't that sweet. We got ourselves a little Cub Scout on our bus."

19

Cub Scout? Terrific, I thought. Skinny Kid chewed on his thumb nail, then turned to look out the window. His face looked so pale I thought the guy might actually disappear.

"Look, it's not a big deal," I said, noticing that Mack had to be a head taller than me. "Just give me the book."

"Not a big deal?" Mack flipped through the handbook, almost like he found it interesting. "Y'all still wear those girly little neck ties and sashes for your badges?"

Mack's little pal turned toward me and started sneezing, again and again, spitting out laughs between them. A whole row away, on the other side of the aisle, and I swear he still got me with his slobber.

I didn't like where Mack was going with this. "So what if it is my handbook," I said. Then I wondered if I might have gotten myself in over my head. I looked at Skinny Kid. Actually, at his back. "Or maybe it's not—"

"What's that? I SAW you trying to hide it!" Mack leaned back in his seat and puffed out his chest.

I looked up front but Alice didn't have a clue what was going on.

"Which is it, new boy?" Then he laughed a fake exaggerated kind of laugh. "You were trying to hide it. You're one of those yellow-bellied losers who hides *eh— va—* thing."

My shoulders kind of jerked; the way he broke the word into syllables, *eh-va-thing,* creeped me out big time. I puffed out my own chest and tried to stare him down.

That's when I noticed a few hairs sticking out of his chin.

How old was this guy?

I tried to imagine what my dad would do.

I waited for Alice to get through a light, so we'd be moving, and then I faced Alice, pretending to see someone I knew at the front of the bus. I smiled and waved at no one.

"Who you waving at, loser?" asked Mack, turning to follow my stare.

It's amazing how fast things can change. In one second, I was leaning into the aisle and pulling the book right out of his hands. The next, he was leaning over and yanking me off my seat and onto the floor. My butt hit hard. Necks stretched over seats; some kids leaned out in the aisle. Everyone wanted to see me, the new kid, sitting on the floor.

I pushed the handbook under me and looked toward Alice. Unbelievable! She was turning a corner and looking out her side window. She hadn't seen a thing.

"You think you're pretty clever now, don't you new boy?" Mack said. "I hope you're in my class. Now get off that book and give it back to me, Cub Scout."

Mack was waiting. Kids were staring. And my butt hurt, bad. But it was weirdly quiet. Why weren't the kids whistling or laughing? Was it Mack? Or were they afraid of Alice? I told myself, take a stand, McDougal. Scouts are proud. Tell him he's the loser for bad mouthing

21

something he's never tried. Tell him! I took a deep breath and—

"Mack Malone." Alice was staring at us in her rear view mirror. Then she stopped the bus and looked over her shoulder. "Don't let me find out you had something to do with our new student sitting on the floor."

Mack spun around. So did everyone else. I guess no one wanted to mess with Alice.

"He didn't," I said, loud enough for Miss Alice to hear. "Just slipped off my seat when you turned." I scrambled back next to Skinny Kid and wedged the book between him and me. Most everyone had already turned to face the front of the bus.

The bus started moving again. I closed my eyes, settled into the hum of the engine, and played out the scene all over again.

Mack tries to pull me out of my seat but I spin around and land a fist in his belly. He can barely breathe. He spits out, "NO!" and doubles over, then puts one hand out to protect himself. But I've already lost interest in him.

I hoped a friendly face might be looking back when I opened my eyes again. I guess everyone had lost interest in me, too. Skinny Kid didn't say a word. I think he nodded once, but it was probably just a bump in the road. So I picked up my sketch pad to get back to my drawing of Mr. August for Dad.

When the bus pulled up in front of DIP, my sketch pad was still blank. Well, except for the word, Dad.

And there stood Mack, waiting by my seat. "You first, Cub Scout."

Chapter 5
Jazz?

We poured off the bus like a waterfall of tee shirts and backpacks—and one very sweaty ironed shirt. I jammed myself in the middle of a bunch of kids, trying to put some distance between Mack and me. My head down, I focused on some guy's high top sneakers. It was so hot. Mostly there was this smell like I was breathing through a mildewed washcloth. But sometimes, a whiff of deodorant or strawberries broke through.

When I looked up from the pack, someone had pushed the fast forward button again. Cars and kids and bicycles were coming from everywhere. Doors slammed. Little kids got out of their parents' cars, wiping off kisses and running into school. Older kids jumped out and walked away, fast. Fast. Fast. Fast.

It might've all freaked me out, but Dad and I had scouted the grounds after that Back-to-School Family Picnic. I knew exactly where to go.

Inside my classroom, all eyes followed my every step. There was a name tag on each desk. Two seats back in what I thought might be my row sat Mack Malone. I read the tags as I headed down my aisle: Malone, Malone, McDougal.

Terrific. Doomed by alphabetical order.

Wait. Two Malones?

A girl headed my way, the one from the bus—the one who maybe had smiled at me. As she passed Mack's desk, he said, "Lookit what the cat dragged in. My dweeb sister, Maggie"

"Shut up, Mack." Maggie Malone slid into the desk in front of me. There was no way those two were twins.

"Psst, Jazz." Maggie looked at a girl to our left. "Psst." Maggie handed her a folded-up note.

Jazz? Hmm.

Jazz palmed the note and looked at me for a split second. And in that split second . . . Zap! An electrical bolt stunned me. She looked away just as fast.

Jazz. Green eyes. Skin—tea color, the way Mom likes it with lots of cream.

Jazz.

She unfolded the paper. She wore rings on every finger. When she leaned over to hide the note, a wall of hair black as a racer snake fell forward. Shiny hair, straight as an arrow. I couldn't stop staring at her. I yelled inside my head, *Look away, McDougal. Don't be a dork.*

I forced myself to face forward just as a lady rushed in. "Sorry, sorry. I'm so late. On the first day of

25

school! Wait. Really? There's no one here? Oh dear. There was a horrible accident on Highway 9 that held up traffic. Did an administrator come by? Someone was supposed to cover for me until I could get here."

"No!" yelled most everyone.

"Oh. Well. My name is Miss Anders." She dumped her purse and briefcase on her desk, smiled, kind of sighed and said, "I'm so happy to be your teacher."

She looked around the room and stopped when she got to me; her eyes were blue, a cool blue, like a swimming pool. Happy eyes. She looked younger than my mom and well, curvier. Kind of pretty for a teacher.

The bell rang and the TV monitor in our classroom showed some kids standing near a flag. One of them said, "Please rise." During the pledge and the announcements, I snuck peeks at Jazz, thinking this day might not be so bad after all.

I had just slid back into my seat, when Miss Anders started calling roll. "Ableman? Mark Ableman?"

My stomach jumped. I hadn't gotten the chance to ask her to call me Spanky. The kids were going to bust a gut when they heard my *real* name.

Miss Anders worked her way through the alphabet. "Dar Garfunkle?"

Skinny Kid raised his hand. "Here."

Dar?

"Well whoop-dee-do. Barf-uncle's in our class," Mack said, just loud enough to get Miss Anders' attention.

"Mr. Malone. You should know that your reputation precedes you. If you have something to say, say it to the whole class."

Mack shot a quick smile at the scrawny kid from the bus. "No, Ma'am," he said. "Got nothing yet this 'mornin."

As Miss Anders continued to call names, I stared at my desk. I kept moving around in my seat. When I realized I was twiddling my thumbs I sat on my hands

"Katy Jefferson?"

Oh man. She was calling Js.

"I'm here!" said a girl near the door.

I could hear Dad telling me, "When one great man dies, another is born to replace him." My underarms were getting sweaty. I wondered for the zillionth time why my parents had to give me *that* name.

"Maya Lopez?"

A girl in the back whispered, "Here."

So what if Grandpa had been an awesome detective. So what if he died the day before I was born! WHO NAMES THEIR KID—

"Mack Malone?"

"Yup."

"Maggie Malone?"

As Maggie raised her hand, I pinched my palm and waited for her to call—

"Sha—"

Miss Anders slapped her forehead and said, "Shame on me. I forgot to introduce our new transfer from Pennsylvania. Mr. McDougal?"

27

Saved! I blew out the breath I'd been holding and shot my hand in the air. "It's Spanky," I said, happy to tell her my nickname. "Here."

All heads turned to face me, including Jazz's. She was smiling. Oh man, I wanted so bad to smile back at her, but not yet. Better to play it cool so she wouldn't think I was some stalker loser and—

"*Spaanky?*" Mack drawled out my name. "Did the new kid just say his name was *Spaanky?*"

Giggles popped around the room. One definitely hit me from Jazz's direction. What an idiot! She wasn't smiling at me. She was about to giggle. I'd been so worried about my real name that I'd forgotten Spanky could sound pretty funny if you hadn't been calling someone that for their whole life like the kids back home.

Miss Anders ignored Mack. I slid low in my seat, closed my eyes, and prayed for my desk and me to break up into particles to transport me back to Pennsylvania.

When she finished calling roll, Miss Anders sat on a high stool near her desk. "During this first six-week term, we're going to be studying Florida wildlife, flora and fauna—all aspects of our outdoor environment."

Flora? Fauna? Huh?

One kid yelled, "What about the campout?"

The class went crazy with everyone talking about some camping trip. One kid yelled, "It's finally our turn!"

"Not now, class. We'll talk about that later." Miss Anders sighed. "Then again, none of you will be able to focus until we do." She pointed to a green area on a

Florida map hanging on a bulletin board. "We'll conclude our study with the annual overnight camping trip in Appalachuway Park. If we succeed in our work, you'll be familiar with your surroundings and able to identify much of what you see."

Lots of kids, including me, clapped. A camping trip? For school? My first grading period was going to be a snap.

"Over the term," she continued, "you will select a topic of interest, research the subject, prepare a report, and present it to the class."

Then again, maybe not.

"No report, no campout."

Over all the moans, Miss Anders added, "Not to worry. You'll have plenty of time. No one's missed the trip yet for *that* reason. We have a lot to cover and I could use some volunteers with camping experience to help me. Anyone?"

A bunch of kids waved their hands.

"I'll do it, Miss Anders."

"Pick me!"

Dar looked at me out of the corner of his eye. No chance he'd raise his hand after the bus incident. But I wasn't just a Scout. Dad and I had taken tons of camping trips. I'd be perfect for the job. Thing was, my arm suddenly felt too heavy to lift.

"Before I pick anyone to be my assistant, I would prefer a volunteer who is an experienced camper," Miss Anders said, scanning the room.

Like me, for instance. My left foot kept tapping the floor and I couldn't sit still. I held on to the corners of my desk closest to Maggie, trying to decide what to do. I almost lifted my right hand to offer. But my fingers ended up drumming the desk instead. Then Mack raised his hand.

"Mack? Are you an experienced camper?" Miss Anders looked surprised.

"Me? Does a wild bear—" But then he eyed me and said, "Not really. What about that new kid? I'm not sure I heard you right—what did you say his name was—*Sppaaanky*? He's a real live Boy Scout, Miss Anders. Little necktie and sash and all. Even carries his handbook to school."

Mack's little pal burst out laughing. Blood rushed to my face, probably adding more freckles. Why hadn't I just left Dar's book on the floor?

Miss Anders' smile disappeared. "Mr. Malone. I would suggest you mind your own business. Spanky is quite capable of volunteering for himself." She looked at me for a second and added "If he chooses to."

I prayed Miss Anders would move on and forget what Mack had said.

"Still, the Boy Scouts I've known have been expert campers," she continued. "Don't you agree, Spanky?"

"Um . . ."

"I'm sure you've been on many campouts, right?" she added.

Every head turned. A zillion eyes were watching me. I had to say something.

30

"See, my dad taught me a lot about camping. What I mean is my dad and I go camping all the time. I mean we *used* to go camping all the time. Up in Pennsylvania. Before we moved here. Before he . . . before he got called . . .I mean, we camped up at Goddard Park, that is, where there's these amazing lakes and tons of cool trails and—"

. Jazz was staring at me, her eyes like full moons. But I couldn't stop jabbering

"—and like my dad would always say when we headed out of town, 'just a straight shot up 'ole Route 79 to heaven' cause he's a firefighter and saves people's lives every day and when he goes. . .when he goes. . . away. . ."

I couldn't remember what I was trying to say.

For a second, all I heard was my heart beat. Then some giggles. My hands slid back and forth along the sides of my thighs. What the heck had I been talking about? I could've just agreed with Miss Anders and said, Yes, Boy Scouts are expert campers. But no. I had to make a big deal about why I'm such a great camper.

". . . So okay, I guess I do have a ton of camping experience."

"Sure sounds like it. Does that mean you'll volunteer to help me?"

Maggie Malone turned around in her desk. Her face went from a blank look to giving me a really quick smile. Then she spun back around. I stared at the top of my desk. The floor wasn't opening. No powerful force was sucking me away through some vacuum tube to some safe place. I had to say something.

"Sure, Miss Anders."

Chapter 6
Seven Measly Days

"How was your day, honey?"

Mom's pale face and zombie stare told me it didn't really matter how I answered. If I could just get her to smile, I thought. "Mom, you're not going to believe it. My bus driver is a gator, my gym teacher is a sting ray and my art teacher is a marlin."

She moved some newspapers from the couch to the coffee table. "What? Oh Spanky. What are you talking about? Did you make any new friends?"

I guess she didn't get my sports team joke. "Not really. This guy Dar—"

But she'd floated off to the kitchen. "Mom?" I followed her. "What's for dinner?"

She opened the fridge and stared inside. "I'm not sure, yet. Dad won't be home."

I guess she forgot what she was looking for 'cause she headed to the sink, leaving the fridge door open. Her eyes looked all watery. "He came home and left again.

Had some things he needed to put in order." She stared out the window. "Nothing for you to be concerned about, Spanky. Do you have homework? That's what you should be focusing on."

Nothing for me to be concerned about? Did she really just say that? Now it was me staring into the fridge, looking for something sweet to get rid of the bad taste in my mouth.

Nothing for me to be concerned about? I grabbed some orange juice and slammed the door shut. "I don't have much homework," I said, and poured a glass. My brain felt like it might shoot out the top of my head. "And I am *concerned*. Whether you want me to be or not!"

Mom turned around. She looked like she was trying to smile. She came over, hugged me and said, "Pizza okay for dinner? Dad will be home before you go to bed. We'll talk some more about it then."

I pulled away, headed back to my room. "Whatever," I said.

After throwing my backpack on my bed, I turned on my computer. I really did have homework, not to mention my Outdoor Ed project to figure out.

Later, some guy delivered a pepperoni pizza. Mom had set up snack tables and put a plate with two slices out for me. The sound of the shower told me I'd be eating by myself. We couldn't afford cable so we only had three channels. There was nothing to watch but news.

Willy the Weather Man pointed to a smiling sun. "More of the same 'H' weather, folks. Haze, heat and humidity."

Yeah, and was his name really Willy or just another "W" word? I was about to get a third piece of pizza from the kitchen when the national news came on. The headline story was another update on the war. A chopper had been shot down.

I changed my mind about more pizza. I'd had enough.

In my room, I did a few math problems and tried to study my first vocabulary list of the year. Somehow I kept ending up on the same word, forgetting what it meant. After trying four thousand times to use it in a sentence, I headed to the shower.

Took my good 'ole time, lathering up, washing my hair. I leaned against the wall, watching the water disappear down the drain.

"Screw you, Army!" I yelled as water beat on my head and rolled down my face, mixing with whatever was coming out of my eyes.

On my way back to my room, I saw my dad sitting on my bed, waiting for me. I tiptoed backward in the hallway so he wouldn't see me. He was rubbing his chin and staring at the calendar he gave me.

"How'd it go today?" he asked, when I walked in.

"Terrific. Great teacher. Her name is Miss Anders. Met a guy named Dar. And at the end of the semester, we're going on an overnight camping trip," I said, getting up the nerve to ask what Mom wouldn't tell me. "So what did you have to put in order? Mom said you had to put something in order. What's that all about?"

Dad patted the bedspread next to him. "Just things soldiers do to make sure their families are protected if something were to happen to them."

"Happen to them?" I dove on the bed. "But we're talking about you, Dad." I sat up and moved next to him. "A long time ago . . . you said you'd be a medic, didn't you? You'll be fine, right?"

"You know it pal." He gave me a quick hug, then put his hands on my shoulders. "That's exactly the way you should be thinking. So—" He got up and took a new black marker from my desk. "I thought you'd want to know the schedule." He stared at my calendar, then put a big X on a date and circled it. I guess for extra effect. When he turned to me, he winked, and said, "That coral snake on the calendar is no friend of Jack's."

I moved to my desk chair to get a closer look at what he'd circled, not caring that he'd remembered the little snake jingle. Seven days away. Seven. Measly. Days.

Dad just shook his head. "We have a lot to cover before I leave."

I smacked the top of my desk. "That's not the way it's supposed to happen. You always said we'd get lots of warning if you ever had to go. Why do you have to leave so soon?"

Dad pulled out the compass he always carried in his pocket, and rubbed it like some genie would magically give him some answers. "Circumstances are different now, son." He sat back on my bed and waved me over.

I didn't budge from my chair. "How are they different?" I gripped the seat. "What changed?"

"A '68 Whiskey' up at Fort Benning got hurt," he said. "They need me to fill his spot."

My brain exploded. "68 whiskey?" I snapped, trying to fight back tears. "What the heck does alcohol have to do with this?"

"That's what the Army calls a combat medic, like me. Remember?"

"How am I supposed to know that?" I asked, flicking a piece of fuzz off my pajama leg. "Okay, so I guess I remember."

Dad stared across the room at my blank walls. "They need me to fill the injured guy's spot. To go through mobilization training with his platoon."

"So. Why? Why now? Can't you wait a few weeks?" No matter how hard I tried to make my voice sound normal, it still sounded whiney. "They'll still be training, won't they?"

Dad flopped back against my pillow. "They're approaching their 'fly window. They'll be scheduling their flights soon to take them . . ."

His lips kept moving but I'd stopped listening. I spun around and around in my chair. I didn't give a snake's rattle about fly windows or mob training. My hands felt shaky and I seriously wanted to punch him to get him to shut up. I'd never felt that way before.

"But you're right, Spank," he said. "It's not how it was supposed to happen. I should have known months ago." Dad's eyes looked tired. He closed them.

"But, but...didn't you say the other day that this war is—"

"—a disaster." His eyes shot open. "I said it was a disaster."

He got up off the bed and headed toward the hallway like I'd made him mad. Served me right. I'd been acting like such a brat; he probably wanted to leave for good.

He stopped at my door and smacked the frame with his hands, hard and loud. Made my body jump. He paced back and forth between my bed and the door. Then he leaned against the wall, shaking his head.

"You can't take that out of context, son. It doesn't matter what I think about the war. I made a commitment."

I dove on my bed and pulled my pillow around my ears. "Whatever," I said, and rolled toward the wall. But when he sat back down on the edge of my bed, I felt a little better, knowing he was still there with me.

"Would you rather me go to prison?" he asked. "That's what happens to soldiers who go AWOL."

He must have wrapped his arm across my back; it felt warm and good. I didn't budge.

"Look, I know this isn't going to be easy for you. We've got a lot to talk about, but it's been a tough day and I'm tired. I promise we'll figure things out before I leave. Just you and me. You know I love you, right?"

Then he hugged me. I wanted to roll over and hug him back so he'd never want to leave. I wanted to hug him so hard he wouldn't be able to leave. But I just stared at the wall.

"Get some sleep, pal."

"But—" My muscles had given up on me. I was too tired to argue. Couldn't even turn over. "Nite Dad," I said, and forced myself to roll back to face him, only he was already gone.

My guts felt like they were in my throat. Or maybe it was the pepperoni pizza. I pulled my pillow against my stomach to stop the ache and stared at the ceiling plaster. It felt like Dad had already gone. I mean, so what if the Army needed him. Mom and I needed him more.

Behind my closed eyes, I saw tanks and explosions from bombs blowing up buildings. And dust, so much dust, clouds of dust and flames and people, people running for their lives. I buried my face in my pillow. But it didn't help. I saw Dad walking through sand dunes. He was dressed like a soldier in fatigues, a helmet. He was carrying a rifle. He had those deep notches between his eyes.

Something was moving in the sand by his boots. A snake! I bolted upright. I started to yell, "Da—," but covered my mouth with my fist and stared at the shadows on the hall wall.

When I heard my mom crying, I curled into a ball and pulled the sheet over my head.

Chapter 7
It Could Happen

On the way to the bus stop the next morning, I forced myself to think about how I'd help Miss Anders teach the class about camping. I knew my way around a campsite and it'd be a way to make some friends, doing something I was pretty good at. That'd be sweet.

As I slipped past Alice on the bus, she winked at me. Mack was sitting in the seat right behind her, wearing his don't-mess-with me look and staring out the window. Dar waved at me to sit next to him. Yeah, the day was getting off to a better start than I'd expected.

I headed to the back and I swear every kid smiled at me. Maybe all of this meant something. Maybe the Army had mixed things up. Maybe they didn't need Dad. Stuff like that happened all the time. The phone could ring and it'd be some General. "Mr. McDougal?" he'd say, "There's been a mistake. We really meant to call a Mr. McDoogan. So go back to work, and give your kid our apology for turning his life upside down."

It could happen.

Every day that week, I headed to the bus stop, believing we'd hear from the Army about the mix up. And every night Dad would come by my room to talk.

One of those nights, I'd been searching the web for stuff on Florida reptiles. Seemed like a good topic for my Outdoor Ed report. Then I realized how many reptiles there were, besides snakes, that is. I'd have to research alligators and crocodiles, iguanas, geckos, skinks, and a dozen different turtles.

I'd just turned around to grab my backpack off my bed and found Dad sitting there. I 'bout had a heart attack.

"Where'd you come from?" I asked.

"Pretty stealthy, huh?" he said, flipping a page on the yellow tablet he was holding. I'm starting a list of things I need you to take care of while I'm away."

And that's how the week went. He reminded me which nights to take the garbage out. "Every Tuesday and Friday, Spanky. I'm counting on you." We talked about lawn mowing, too. Then he X'd off a square on my calendar.

As the week wore on, he'd remember something else. Helping Mom with the laundry, cleaning up after dinner—stuff like that. I'd shake my head as if I was paying close attention. We walked around the garage so he could remind me where he kept his tool box, extra batteries, and light bulbs.

I'd say, "I know, Dad. I know."

And he'd X off another square.

On Wednesday, he pulled me back to the garage to show me how the safety valve worked on the lawn mower's gas can. He even thought he had to show me how to use a plunger. Sheesh. And that night, he X'd out square #3.

I wanted to talk to him about Mack. About how, every day Mack found a way to remind me that he wasn't done with me—shoving me into my locker, tripping me on the bus, giving me a cold stare and pointing his finger at me as I passed him in the hall. Dad would help me figure out what to do. But everything else seemed more important. And there'd been no apology call from the Army.

On Thursday night, Mom's crying woke me up. I tried to drown it out by hugging my pillow around my head and humming, but her voice got louder. "Tell me you'll come home after training, before you go overseas."

"Shhhh...don't cry..." was all I could hear Dad say.

"I can't help it. I'm so afraid something will happen to you."

I threw off my covers, stormed into my bathroom and flicked on the light. Squinting, my reflection stared back at me. What the heck did Mom think was going to happen? Dad was a firefighter and an EMT. He'd saved people from dying practically every single day since I'd been born. He was a real life hero. He could handle anything.

I knew Mom couldn't help how sad she got. How she stayed in bed all day sometimes. Thing was, Dad could usually cheer her up, but not so much that night. How was I supposed to cheer her up with him gone?

I splashed cold water on my face and on my way back to bed, I peeked in on them. They were sitting in shadows. The only light was coming from the kitchen. There was a bottle of beer on the coffee table. Mom sat on one end of the couch; she had her knees up, her arms wrapped around them, and she was rocking back and forth. She looked like a scared little kid.

Dad was sitting next to her, his arm around her shoulder. He moved the pen and paper he'd been holding to the coffee table and hugged her.

I tiptoed back to my room, tried to fall back asleep. Only I kept seeing Mom on the couch, rocking back and forth.

Chapter 8
Try Not To Get Upset

The next day, I came home from school to the smell of Mom's Crock Roast with potatoes and carrots and home-made biscuits. That's what she called pot roast cooked in a crock pot. Ha, ha. The smell of garlic and onions reminded me of my grandparent's house when they were alive . . . when we were back home and my life was normal.

Dad was leaving for training in the morning. He'd been running around, fixing things, packing, and making more lists all day. The guy was totally wired.

I had to talk to him about Mack. If I was going to talk to him, it had to be that night.

Dinner started out quiet. We all were wolfing down mom's roast, but nothing tasted right to me. Then Dad announced "Let's make some plans for when I get back."

Mom smiled. Yeah, good move, Dad.

He smiled back, and said, "Promise me you'll make another meal like this one. That'll give me something delicious to look forward to."

Mom's face went blank. So he looked at me. "What about you?"

"How about you and I go on one of our camping trips. But next time, I'll find our way back when we get lost in the woods."

I don't know what I'd said wrong but Mom's face went from blank to looking like she might start crying again. She blurted out, "I'm sorry, I have to go get—" and then ran to the kitchen.

Dad said, "You're on, pal." He got up and headed in her direction, but looked back to say, "We'll have to pick a new forest, though. Maybe the one you're going to on that Outdoor Ed. trip."

As I waited for them to come back, I flicked bread crumbs across the table. The half-eaten Crock Roast looked like dog food. Nice memory to leave Dad with, I thought. I peeked into the kitchen, hoping to find them but it was empty. So after I loaded the dishwasher, I watched water swirl down the sink drain.

I had one night left with Dad until he got back from training.

I was already in bed waiting for him when he came by my room. He X'd out the last calendar square and when he sat on the edge of my bed, he looked more tired than I'd ever seen him.

"So here's the list of all the things I need you to take care of." Then he handed over his yellow pad. "All the things we've talked about."

I pretended to read it, my head bobbing up and down, but it looked like a jumble of letters and lines. "Sure Dad. Not a problem."

"Remember while I'm in training, we'll be able to talk and email. After I ship out, I just don't know exactly how that will work yet. But we'll figure it out a day at a time."

"Sure Dad." I put his list on my night table. "I was wondering if I could talk to you about—"

"About your mom," he said, and handed me an envelope. "You know we don't have a lot of money, Spanky. But I've always saved some for special occasions. Keep it tucked away somewhere—for emergencies. If Mom's having a tough day, buy her a flower. Or some malted milk balls. You know how much she likes malted milk balls. A little surprise won't fix things, but it'll help."

"Sure Dad. I can do that."

Dad pushed out his lower lip. "I know you can. Look. I don't know how to say this. Mom can't help it when she gets down— what I'm trying to say is how sometimes— what I mean is, her sadness is real. But she always gets through it."

I thought, yeah, with you around. But what about when you're gone? "Sure Dad, but I—"

"Talk to her. Try not to get upset with her if she gets sad. Okay?"

In my head, I whined, do we have to keep talking about Mom? What about me? But then I felt like a jerk.

Dad had too many things to worry about without me adding to it.

"It's okay. You don't have to tell me, Dad. I know." I bit my lip to keep from saying anything else.

***

I woke up in a cold sweat. Dad had left and I hadn't gotten to say goodbye to him. I threw off my sheet and ran to the window, expecting his truck to be gone.

The smell of coffee pulled me to the kitchen; Mom and Dad were sitting at the counter. The clock read 6:00 am. Dad looked it—tee shirt, undershorts, lots of stubble. Mom had on a yellow dress but she looked like she hadn't slept in a month.

I yawned. "You guys stay up all night?"

Dad leaned back in his chair and looked at me for the longest time; he was smiling in that weird way, the way he would smile after he'd shown me how to do something and I got it right the first time. "Want a cup of my famous coffee?"

"Um, no Dad. I don't really drink coffee, remember? What time do we have to leave?"

He looked at Mom but didn't say anything.

"No way," I said. "You don't get to leave without me going with you. I don't care if it's a school day." The words hadn't exactly come out the way I wanted. "I want to go to the airport with you."

Dad kept staring at me. Finally, he said, "We don't have to leave until 9:30, so how about I fix you one of my famous waffles?"

I loved his waffles drenched in syrup. And I really wanted to spend every last minute with him. But the truth was, I suddenly just wanted to go back to sleep.

I took the waffle iron out of the pantry and plugged it in while Dad melted some butter. Then he mixed it with egg yolks and club soda. "That's the secret to crisp, light waffles," he said, and added a bunch of other stuff. "Club soda. You following me?"

"Yep." I wondered if he really expected me to remember what he was saying. "So, Dad. After your training and, you know, before you ship out—"

"Hang on to that thought. Here, you do it." He handed me a big ladle. I scooped some batter and poured it on the open waffle iron. "Now close it," he said. "Wait for the steam to quit."

Neither of us said anything. Whiffs of steam escaped. "So Dad, like I'm saying, maybe after your training, when you come home before you go overseas, you and I could pitch a tent in the backyard. You know. One last campout before you hit the desert."

Dad stared off to some far-away place. He pulled a chair away from the table, spun it around and sat on it backwards. With his elbows resting on the chair back, he ran his hands through his hair. Not the reaction I was looking for.

I asked him what was wrong but he didn't say anything and the steam coming out of the waffle iron

48

had stopped. He got up, opened the iron, lifted he waffle with a fork, and put it on a plate for me.

I smothered it with syrup. "So . . . what do you think, Dad?" I stabbed a chunk, watched the syrup drip off, caught a string of it with my tongue and then shoved the piece in my mouth, talking as I chewed. "About camping in the back yard."

"Look. I thought you understood, Spanky. I'll be heading overseas right from Fort Stewart. I won't be able to come home for a visit."

"But—"

"I know. I know. I would have been able to come home under normal circumstances. But like I said the other night—I'm filling a spot. There's no time. Remember?"

"I guess." I started to take another bite but the waffle and syrup suddenly seemed too sweet. Plus, there must have been something in it that made me way sleepy. "Is it okay if I go back to bed for a little while?"

"Sure, pal. I've got some last-minute packing to do anyway. And Spanky—"

I turned back. "Yeah, Dad?"

"I'm not going to be gone forever. We'll get through this. Right?"

I was back in bed before I realized I'd never answered him.

Chapter 9
A Soldier's Son

The Army was nice enough to buy Dad a plane ticket to the training base in Savannah. Good 'ole Army. For some reason, he wanted the truck windows open on the way to the airport. Maybe to get used to the heat where he was going? Or to feel the wind in his hair with no helmet on? The sun was blazing. Personally, I wanted to wipe it right out of the sky. Didn't seem right that it should be shining.

It usually takes about two hours to get to the Tampa airport. But the airport signs started popping up way too fast. Seemed like we'd just left the house. Dad drove up the ramp and pulled into the short-term parking garage. He found a parking space immediately.

The fast forward button was on again.

When we got out of the truck, Mom and I probably looked like the living dead from some horror movie. Dad looked like a giant in his fatigues, in those tan Army boots. I wanted the boxers and scruffy-bearded dad back.

Inside, he set down his duffle and stared in the direction of the security checkpoint. "You want to know why I have to go overseas?" His voice sounded angry, like he was mad at me or at the Army or maybe even the world. He nodded at the guards. "You know what they're doing, don't you Spanky? They're checking for weapons and explosives. All because of those terrorists."

A bunch of soldiers nearby must've been going to the same place as Dad. One was saying goodbye to two little kids who were busy hugging their mom's legs. She was smiling—the same smile Mom had over the past few days, about as real as a Halloween mask. A lady soldier was holding some guy's hand. I forgot soldiers could be girls.

The soldier with the little kids had tears rolling down his cheeks. None of the other soldiers cried.

Mom tugged at Dad and me. "I need to find a restroom. Don't go anywhere, okay?"

As soon as she left, Dad bent down on one knee. He looked up, and said, "It's going to be a great year for you, Spanky. New school. New friends, right?"

"Sure, Dad."

He hugged me quick and hard. "I have something important to say, so let me talk and don't interrupt, okay?"

I nodded.

"Since the day you were born you've been my son." His voice cracked. "But with me going to war, that makes you a soldier's son. You understand that makes you the man of the house for a while."

51

I guess that's what every soldier tells his son. My head must've looked like one of those bobble-headed dolls. My eyes were burning. I nodded again, trying hard not to cry. If Dad and most of those other soldiers weren't crying, I sure as heck wasn't going to.

Then Dad put something in my hand and wrapped his huge hands around mine. They felt strong and warm. Like another hug. "My dad gave me this when I was your age. I want you to have it. Always came in handy for me when I lost my way."

I opened my palm to find his compass. I couldn't believe he was giving it to me. I pulled a folded up piece of paper from my back pocket and gave it to him.

Dad opened it and studied it for a minute. Then he smiled, and said, "The rings are in the right order. You remembered. This little guy is no friend of Jack's!" Then he looked me straight in the eyes. "I'm going to need you to be strong for me, son."

My throat closed up. Made it hard to get the words out. "Not a problem, Dad."

"Remember what we talked about last night, about Mom? Help her as best you can, okay?"

I nodded again. "We'll be okay, Dad. Just you be okay, okay?"

His eyes looked watery, but he turned his head real fast. "Listen son. For some reason, you and your mom put me up on some crazy pedestal. But here's the truth. The only way I'm able to leave like this, without completely going out of my mind, is that I know I can count on you."

"I got it covered, Dad. Don't worry about a thing."
A stomach cramp doubled me over. I wanted to run to
the bathroom. Instead, I kneeled down next to him.

We must've looked pretty funny, both of us on our
knees. Dad jabbed at my nose, pretending to box with
me. I put up my fists to block him, then jabbed at his
chin. He bonked my head—what he called a C.O.D—*a
conk on the donk*, and said, "I guess it's your turn to be
the hero for a while."

"Yeah." I couldn't help but roll my eyes. "As if."

He smiled. "I love you, son. I'll be fine. We'll all be
fine. And I'll be back before you know it."

Mom came back so we stood up. Dad gave me
another quick hug, then took Mom's hand and the two
of them walked away. He put his arms around her so I
looked down, scuffed the carpet with the toe of my shoe,
and counted the chairs in the waiting area, waiting for
them to finish saying goodbye.

When it was time, Mom stood behind me with her
hands resting on my shoulders. Dad untied his boots
and set them on the conveyor belt. He put his duffle bag
next to his shoes and we watched them pass through
the x-ray machine. Dad walked through the security
arch and then put his boots back on.

He waved one last time. Mom and I watched 'till he
was out of sight.

"Let's go home, Spanky." Her voice sounded so
tired. We headed toward the doors to the garage.

"Spanky!"

I looked back. Dad had turned around and was running back to the security checkpoint.

I yelled, "What's up?" wondering what he'd forgotten.

His face looked as serious as I'd ever seen it. He wasn't smiling anymore or jabbing at me or teasing me about being a hero. He just looked me dead in the eyes for what felt like forever. Then he turned again, looked over his shoulder, and said, "Make me proud of you."

Chapter 10
Pretend

Outside the cafeteria window, it looked like the Fat Guys had finished unloading their van. The rain kept falling and I felt empty. Just as empty as that day we'd dropped Dad at the airport. But not as empty as I felt on the way home.

Mom shouldn't have been driving that day. She gripped the steering wheel so hard, her fingers looked white. For the first thirty minutes, she cried on and off. But then she stopped and it got quiet. The kind of quiet that can choke you.

The truck seemed emptier without him. It wasn't just his body that was missing. The air seemed sucked out, too.

"A year will fly by, right Mom?" Talking helped me breathe easier. "Before you know it, Dad'll be home again."

Mom's head bobbed and her eyes got watery again. I watched for cars slowing down in front of us, praying she saw them. I pointed out stop signs and red lights. I wished I was old enough to drive. "And like Dad said, we'll talk on the phone and send emails and stuff."

The trip home dragged. How could it seem to go so fast on the way to the airport, but take forever on the way back? Miles of boring road and empty billboard signs. A dead dog in the road. It wasn't pretty. Made me wonder what he was thinking before he got hit. Was he a pup? Or a Dad?

At home Mom went back to bed. Said she hadn't slept much the night before. "I'm guessing you didn't either," she said, and hugged me.

With Mom asleep, I had the house to myself, which could've been a cool thing if the place didn't feel so empty. It started raining, but this time bolts of lightning lit up the house and the thunder boomed loud. I kept thinking it could break the windows. I grabbed my snake book and dove on the couch, but I couldn't concentrate. The hum of the refrigerator motor got on my nerves. The air-conditioning sounded like a wind storm, and I jumped every time the icemaker clunked out new cubes. I couldn't believe how noisy this new house was—I wanted everything to just shut up.

Then, as if someone had hit a huge OFF button, every noise stopped all at once. It was quiet—a heavy kind of quiet that made it hard to stay awake. I nodded off.

When I woke up later, I wanted to fix something to eat. Found a can of spaghetti in the pantry, pulled the tab on the top to open it and poured it into a bowl. I was

P.S. We can tough it out, right? You and me? I know we can!

I wrote him back immediately,

Dear Dad,
You made it! Glad you are AOK. Guess what? That storm you flew through took out our power. I ate cereal for dinner. Oh and Dad, I didn't get to talk to you last night about this guy at my school.

In the time it took to figure out how to tell him about Mack, I changed my mind. If he was worried about me and Mack, maybe he'd miss something important in his training. So I erased the last two lines and wrote:

Mom and I ate cereal for dinner! Write me every day, okay?
Love,
Spanky

Dad had a few more weeks of training before he headed to the Middle East. I kept his compass in my pocket every day and on my night table when I got home. We sent emails back and forth, and talked on the phone a lot. I guess we were both just trying to get used to all of it.

He'd say how much he missed me. I'd tell him I wished he was home. He'd talk about the training. I'd say it couldn't be too tough for him. Then I'd tell him something good about Mom or school and that I was taking care of everything just fine. I left out anything about Mack.

It was like we were in a play. He had the part of the tough soldier. I was the brave kid at home. I wondered if that was what the Army wanted me to do.

Pretend.

Chapter 11
Spunky Spanky

Half asleep, I shuffled into the kitchen the next morning, threw a frozen waffle in the toaster and plopped in a chair to wait it out. Maybe it was the smell of the waffle, but it reminded me of Saturday mornings back up north. Neighbors would stop by and drink coffee with Dad.

Wouldn't hurt if I could make kids feel that way. Like they wanted to hang with me.

The kitchen table was covered with all kinds of stuff: Newspapers, mail, flyers. Reading the comics seemed like a good time killer until a yellow envelope sticking out from under the paper became more interesting. It looked official, maybe Army papers. Probably would have torn it to shreds if I hadn't seen the return address—The David I. Patrick School—and the envelope was addressed to Spanky McDougal and his Parents

My heart flipped backwards. Had I done something wrong? I ripped it open and found a bunch of papers, including a green flyer that said:

The David I. Patrick Middle School
Annual Outdoor Education
OVERNIGHT CAMPING TRIP - Appalachuway Park
Less than six weeks away.
Be prepared!

Be prepared? Man, was I ever!

We studied Outdoor Ed. twice a week. That
morning, Miss Anders let us use our books on the
Florida Environment to make lists of plant species we
might find on the trails. I drew a little sketch by each
one I picked.

Turns out flora are plants and fauna are the
critters. Besides snakes, I found out I might actually get
to see bobcat, gray fox, white-tailed deer, flying
squirrels, owls and woodpeckers. I couldn't believe this
was school work!

At lunch, as I unwrapped my bologna and
mustard sandwich, there was no mistaking Dar's
vocabulary as he rounded the end of the table and sat
down. "So, care to tell me the origin of your nickname?"

"The origin?" I crumpled the wrapper from my
lunch and tossed it in the garbage can by the wall. "My
dad gave it to me when I was a little kid, right after my
first haircut. He thought I looked like this kid, Spanky,
in an old television show."

"Let me guess. The Our Gang film shorts," Dar
said. "Circa late 1920's. Am I correct?"

I had no clue, but I nodded.

Dar's eyes got all fired up just like his voice. "They were originally silent films. MGM added sound, but it wasn't until the 50's that they aired on television."

The guy was a walking, talking fact-mobile. But then he dropped his chin and rolled his eyes up to look at me. "So, did you know that show is hardly PC anymore?"

PC? The guy was seriously starting to bug me. "What's PC?"

"Politically Correct. Some find a few of the episodes highly offensive. When was the last time you watched it?"

"Actually," I said, shaking my head. "I haven't seen any of the shows since I was a little kid."

That was all I needed. Back home, my name was just an old nickname that no one paid any attention to. Here, it wasn't PC, and I was probably upsetting someone without saying a word.

"Anyway," I added, "my dad and I used to watch that show. I guess he hoped I'd turn out like the TV Spanky—kind of spunky. Not afraid to do things."

As Dar blabbed on about some of the actors, I thought about that word. Spunky. Not afraid. Yeah, just like my dad. I could be spunky, too, right?

I mean, why not? That would make my dad proud!

Chapter 12
Ms. Badoo-doo

A few days had gone by after Dad left. When the bell rang first thing, a lady who wasn't Miss Anders walked in. She looked around the room, her head bouncing up and down as it swept from one side of the room to the other.

"Good *Morrrrning* my children." she said. "My name is Ms. Badu. That's baaah like a sheep and do like how doooo you do! I'll be your substitute teacher for today."

She looked and sounded like no other sub I'd ever had. Her voice was deep. It kind of moved through my ears along my veins and down to the pit of my stomach. Made me feel happy. Weird.

I couldn't help staring. She was big, spread out like the queen on a deck of cards or something. Her face and arms reminded me of smooth chocolate pudding and her lips were puffy and fire-engine-red. Her dress looked like a rainbow ocean—waves of red, blue, and yellow. The rainbow was wrapped around her head, too, like a beehive.

Mr. Blowford, our principal waddled in. "Good morning, ladies and gentlemen."

Blowford reminded me of a zoo in human form: frog voice, duck feet that pointed outward instead of straight forward, and a puffed out chest like a blowfish. Either the guy had a closet full of three-piece brown suits or he wore the same one every day to match his brown, old-geezer tie-up shoes. He definitely must have time-traveled to Appalacheeville from some other decade.

"Miss Anders will be out all morning for a doctor's appointment. Class, this is Ms. Badu."

"Hmmm. Hmmm. Hmmm," Ms. Badu hummed. She looked around the room, smiling like she'd won the lottery or something, and when her eyes passed by me, they pulled a smile right out of me. Seriously weird.

Blowfish, I mean Mr. Blowford and Ms. Badu sorted through the papers on Miss Anders' desk. Then Mr. Blowford held up Miss A's grade book. "While Ms. Badu looks over the lesson plans," he said, "I shall call the roll."

Before he got to Mack's name, I was a sweaty mess. He'd be calling my name any minute. My real name. There was no hiding it this time. I readied my hand to get his attention.

Soon enough, Mr. Blowford called out, "Maggie? Maggie Malone?"

Just as Maggie said, "Here," I shot my hand up, fast like a torpedo, to tell him I'm next, to tell him to call me Spanky, to beg him not to call me—

"Shamus? Shamus McDougal?" Blowfish never looked up.

Mack spun around to me and blurted out, "Shamus? Did he just call you Shamus?"

The other kids were looking around the room, giggling. My mouth felt like I had sucked on a lemon.

Blowfish shouted, "Shamus McDougal?"

Mack turned back to Blowfish. "He *did* call you Shamus!"

I whispered, "Yes, sir," and raised my hand the way you raise a flag after something bad happens—at half-mast. I could barely hear myself over the laughter.

Blowfish puffed out his chest and barked, "That'll be enough out of all of you. Shamus is a fine name. My dearly departed wife's father went by the name of Shamus."

Dar blurted out, "He goes by Spanky, Mr. Blowford."

Blowfish said, "Mr. McDougal, I will be happy to call you Spanky, and as for you Mr. Malone, we're barely into the school year and you are already testing my patience."

Ms. Badu whispered something to Blowfish. He nodded. "I will leave you in the expert hands of Ms. Badu," he said, and left.

Ms. Badu looked around the room again and her happy eyes pulled another smile out of me. How did she do that?

"Hey Ms. Badoo-doo," Mack called out. "What's wrong with Miss Anders?"

She stared out the window for a few seconds and in that deep, deep voice she said, "I have a hunch we have some very special students in this class." Then she whipped her head toward Mack. In a not so happy voice, she said, "Let's start with you. Tell me your name again, son."

The room went silent. All you could hear was the clock over the white board. Tick. . .tick. . .tick. . .

Ms. Badu's body was so wide, when she walked down our aisle, her dress polished the desks on both sides. She stopped right in front of me! I swear she smelled like homemade cookies. But then she turned so she was looking at the back of Mack's head. Mack stared at the GI Joe comic book lying open on his desk.

Tick. . .tick. . .tick. . .

The clock was beginning to sound like a bomb. Finally, Mack turned to look up at her. "Mack. My name is Mack Malone." He pushed his hair off his forehead, and then crossed his arms in front of his chest for his don't-mess-with-me pose.

"Well Mr. Mack Malone. Stand right up and let me take a goooood look at you."

Mack slapped his comic book shut and took his good 'ole time standing up.

Ms. Badu didn't even flinch. She looked him over and said, "Now class, Mr. Mack Malone is a verrry special young man. He's also a verrry concerrrned young man who wants to know what's wrong with Miss Anders."

The rest of us who sat close to Mack watched his face turn from pink to red.

"In fact," Ms. Badu said, talking all sweet-like, "Mr. Verrry Special Mack Malone is so concerned, he forgot to raise his hand and wait to be called upon."

She took a few steps toward the front. But then she stopped. She looked over her shoulder, lowered her head a little, and cocked her eyebrow. "Now, isn't that right Mr. Malone?"

There was that not-so-sweet voice again. She glared at him over the upper rim of her glasses. So much for happy eyes.

Mack's face was looking more like a tomato. "Yes. I mean no. I mean, I don't know."

"Miss Anders had a doctor's appointment. Beyond that, it's none of your business, son."

She turned to the whiteboard and wrote "Ms. Badu" in large curvy letters. The marker must've been running out of ink 'cause you couldn't see the "u" With her back to us, Ms. "Bad" said, "Mr. Mack Malone, put that comic book away and remember your manners from now on."

Mack slowly slid it under his desk, rolling his eyes big time.

Miss Badu made us review Chapter 2 in our math books. Decimals. Not fun. Afterwards, Miss Anders' lesson plans said if we had time, we could talk about camping to get us up to speed for our trip.

"Have any of you been camping before?" Ms. Badu asked. "I'm sure we have a few experts in this group."

Like me for instance. Whoa. Maybe Miss A wrote something down about me helping.

"All of you take out a blank sheet of paper."

Then again, maybe not.

She wrote THE MOST IMPORTANT on the white board. But the red marker faded to nothing. "Hang on a minute," she said, searching through her rainbow colored purse. She pulled out a huge purple marker, went back to the board, and finished writing

THE MOST IMPORTANT THINGS I NEED TO KNOW ABOUT CAMPING.

"Let's shake things up a little bit in here. Each of you pick a partner. Camping takes teamwork. So let's see how well you work in teams."

Mack gave Ned a high five.

"All wight!" Ned said.

Everyone in the room paired off. I looked over at Jazz, but Maggie had moved to an empty desk behind hers. Dar liked to work by himself. There was only one kid left. Otie. The guy who I figured had to have been allergic to deodorant. He stared at the seat next to mine.

"I guess it's you and me, Otie" I said. He seemed relieved and moved over an aisle.

Sure enough, Dar raised his hand. "Would it be acceptable if I work by myself? I prefer to fly solo."

"You're Mr. Garfunkle, am I right?"

"That would be Dar Garfunkle," Dar said, with a big smile on his face.

"My, oh my, aren't you a cool cucumber? And you sound like a rather intelligent young man." Ms. Badu's eyes changed from happy to well, not. She got closer to his face, and said, "But I said I want to see you all work together. You did hear me say that now didn't you?"

"Yes ma'am, but . . ." Dar kind of jerked his head back. I'm guessing he wasn't exactly used to having a teacher give him a hard time.

"I'm not interested in buts," she added, heading back to her desk and pointing at Mack. "Now why don't you move over there next to Ned and Mack? The three of you pull your desks together. In fact, let's have some fun this morning. The first team to list ten important things you need to know about camping gets to do something special."

Ned whispered, "Dang! Maybe we'll get a pwize with Bwain Sludge on aw team."

There was a knock on the door. Blowfish stuck his head in again and motioned for Ms. Badu to step out into the hall. Dar had been scribbling away 'cause when the door closed, he announced, "I'm done. Let's compare answers." That was Dar for you. Too smart and too fast to ever work with anyone in class.

"We ain't got nothing yet," Ned said. "Come on, Dar. Give us what ya got so we can win."

"Excuse me?" Dar glared at them. "I think not."

I should've been working on my own list, but I couldn't help listening in. "Listen Four-Eyes, we're a team. So you gotta give us your answers."

Dar turned his paper over. "I believe I said no."

Mack reached over to grab it, but Dar pushed his hand away. In three quick moves, Mack stood up, swiped Dar's paper, and slapped it on Ned's desk. Then he yanked Dar's arm, pulling him out of his seat and onto the floor.

My shoulder ached a little, as if Mack had thrown me on the floor. I should do something, I thought, but Dar had pulled himself back into his desk and wrapped his arms across his stomach. "Leave me alone, Malone."

Still standing, Mack turned to Ned and raised his hand for a high-five. Ned slapped it the exact same moment that Ms. Badu came back in.

Chapter 13
"P" Stands for Pansy

Flashing one of her big smiles at Mack and Ned, Ms. Badu said, "You boys must be finished, since you're not sitting in your desks. I will assume the three of you are ready with your answers."

"Yes ma'am," Mack said, scrambling into his seat to copy Dar's paper.

"It appears we have ourselves a winner! Your prize is to be the teacher this morning. Professor Malone, let's start with you."

Ned blurted out, "That's aw sawpwise?"

"Come on up here, Professor Malone—right here beside me," said Ms. Badu. "I want you to lead the class in a discussion about the MOST important thing you'll need to know to have a successful camping trip."

"Professor? More like Neanderthal loser," whispered Dar. Problem was he whispered it at the exact same moment Ms. Badu had stopped talking. The look she gave him sent him slumping in his seat.

Mack stared at his mostly blank paper. He shrugged, then shuffled up to the front of the class.

I couldn't believe it. I was supposed to be helping Miss Anders. But no. And now Mack was going to teach the class about camping? First he's rude to Ms. Badu, then he throws Dar around and she lets him lead the class? Suddenly, I didn't like this sub. I didn't like her at all.

Mack looked at Dar. Then at Ms. Badu. Then at me. "Well then. Being the teacher and all, I think I'll pick a couple of y'all to come up here. Mr. McDorkal and Mr. Barf Uncle."

Ms. Badu was in Mack's face just as he finished saying the second Mr. "I guess if I'm going to ask you to be the teacher," she said, "I shouldn't judge how you play the part. But I will not have any name calling. Understood?"

Mack shrugged. I grabbed my worksheet, but of course, it was blank. Otie tried to hand me his sheet, but heck, I could've written the list in my sleep.

The "professor" gave me a marker. "So Boyyy Scout," he said, snapping his head to look at Ms. Badu. "I'm not calling him any names, Ms. Badu. Honest. He really is a Boy Scout. In the flesh. Little neck tie. Sash too. I swear!" Then he turned back to me. "I'm 'bettin your BOY SCOUT MANUAL told you what the MOST important camping skill is, 'bein that you ARE a BOY SCOUT and all."

Ms. Badu shook her head and handed me her purple marker. "Use mine," she said, as she walked to the back of the room.

Facing the board, a zillion scouting memories shot through my head.

Tick . . . tick . . . tick. . .

What was the MOST important thing?

Tick . . . tick . . . tick. . .

Then it hit me. Something my old scout leader had told us over and over that never really sunk in until that very moment. None of our camping trips would've been as much fun if we hadn't prepared in advance. PREPARATION was THE most important part of camping.

Feeling a little spunky, I slid the marker across the board forming a big "P". Preparation. Just like Dad and I were doing before he—

Before he—

Before he—before he heads to some desert to fight in some stupid war. All of a sudden, right then and there, it got real. Too real. My hand started shaking. My eyes got blurry and my legs felt wobbly. Spunky? Hah. A sour taste squirted in my mouth, the one you get right before you're going to puke.

And the "P" was waiting for me to finish.

Tick . . . tick . . . tick. . .

My mind had gone blank. I had nothing.

Mack pushed me aside. "P? Is that all you can come up with, McDougal?" He whispered, "Pansy. That's it. The P stands for Pansy. You know. Just like you!" He ripped the marker out of my hand. "Let a real soldier help you," he said in a voice loud enough for the whole class to hear. Then he finished my sentence with "PUT UP A TENT."

"It's pitch," I said, seeing what he wrote. "You don't put up a tent. You pitch a tent. And for the record, that's not what I was going to write."

I tried to take the marker from him to write preparation, but he took a big step backwards. I ended up grabbing at nothing but air.

Meanwhile, Ms. Badu was headed back up front. "Professor Malone," she said. "I see you and Mr. McDougal have put your heads together and come up with an answer. Put up a tent. Well, I guess that's one important part of camping."

But before I could correct her, she looked at me and kind of took a double-take. "Are you feeling all right, Spanky? You look a little pale."

"No ma'am," I answered. "I'm not feeling so hot. Is it okay if I sit down?"

She nodded for me to go back to my seat and went back to smiling at Mack. I sat down, put my head on my desk, and prayed that the Badoo-doo lady wouldn't be back the next day.

Chapter 14
I'll Kick Your Little. . .

Back then, right after Dad had left, I'd finally gotten to rip off the page on my calendar all marked up with big Xs. I was hoping the change in months would give Willy the Weatherman a new letter to describe things, say maybe C words like cool and comfortable. But no, he'd be sticking with his H words.

There wasn't a breath of air. It was as if someone called Red Light, STOP and the world froze. Or maybe some big fan in the sky that moves air around the earth broke. Every leaf on every limb was still. Even the birds looked like they were painted on their perches. Nothing moved.

As I headed to the back of the bus one morning, Alice grabbed my arm. "Hold on, Spanky. Why don't you sit up here with me today?"

"Thanks, but I need to talk to—"

In the back of the bus, Mack had jammed Dar up against the window. Our eyes connected, Mack's and mine, and I knew he was trying to freak me out. Dar too. Just like that first day on the bus.

Miss Alice pointed to the row behind her. "Right here, Spanky."

"Um. . . I should probably go back and help—" I searched the rows for an empty seat that both Dar and I could sit in. Every seat had at least one person in it. Worse yet, in the back, there was only one seat on the other side of the aisle from Mack.

"Spanky, do yourself a favor and sit here." Alice shoved a shopping bag off the seat, and then put the bus in gear.

"So how do you like your new school, Spanky?" she asked.

It was hard to hear over the road and engine noises so I leaned in closer. "Pretty well."

"Made any friends, yet?"

"Yeah, I guess. Dar Garfunkle."

"Mr. Vice President Al Gore's buddy! Smart boy, that Dar."

I had no idea what she was talking about. But before I could ask, she said, "So you're from Pennsylvania. I hear it's pretty up there."

I nodded.

"I know, I know. I'm a nosey old hoot. I just like to know all about the kids on my bus. Now your mom and dad. How do they like our little town?"

"All right, I guess," I said, starting to feel a little antsy.

"Does your Mom travel? Or your old man? Is he the traveling kind of dad? Or is he more of a homebody? I always worry about those kids whose parents have to be away."

She was right about the nosey thing. I got a bad taste in my mouth, wondering if she somehow knew about Dad leaving. I mean, why was she asking me that?

I shoved my hand in my pocket and rubbed Dad's compass. I didn't have to talk about it, did I? "You don't have to worry about me, ma'am," I said, and sat back, hoping she'd get the hint.

Maybe it was the warm breeze and the rumble of the bus, or the fact that I hadn't slept that well the night before, but the next thing I knew we were at school. Mack must have rushed up to the front because when I opened my eyes, he was standing next to my row, holding out his arm.

"After you, McDougal," he said, and smiled at Alice.

A line of kids waited behind him, so I had to get up. I flexed every muscle in my body as I climbed down the bus steps, knowing he was right behind me. When my foot hit the ground a hand clamped on my shoulder and a black boot landed next to my sneaker.

"Hey McDougal. Wait up." His friendly voice didn't match the vice grip he had on me. A few steps later, out of Alice's hearing range, he said, "Paint a smile on your face, McDougal! Now!"

"Huh?" But Mack tightened his grip even harder, so I smiled.

"Way to kiss up to Alice, new boy."

"I wasn't—"

His voice got louder with each step. "Keep that smile on your face, you fruity little Cub cake. If you ever squeal to Alice—or to anyone about me, I swear I'll kick your little—"

Mr. Blowford came out of nowhere. "Good morning, boys. That's good of you to get to know our new student, Mack."

Mack let go. I nodded, still smiling. "Gotta run," I said, and then ran inside the building.

When Mack got to class, he didn't say a word. He didn't speak to anyone really. He just walked up to my desk, clenched his fist, and pounded the top of my desk, once, hard. Then he put his fist on the tip of my nose, and shoved me back in my seat. The whole time, he didn't say a word. Seemed way too quiet.

Quiet like a hand grenade.

I tried to forget about Mack by secretly eyeing Jazz. She was a lefty. Just like me! I couldn't stop looking at her sparkly rings. Her hand curled around a pencil and she was sketching what looked like Miss Anders' face. I had to figure out a way to make my move.

I watched her stand up and face the flag. As she said the pledge, ". . . allegiance to the flag..." I pretended she was saying it to me.

So far, all I knew about her was that she liked to paint. We both had art in the afternoon and since I sketched snakes, I figured it gave us something in common. Only she was on the Monday and Wednesday

79

schedule. And me? I had art on Tuesday and Thursday. Mr. Riley had hung some of her amazing drawings on the wall in the art room. They were mostly pictures of faces—a couple from our class. One looked a little like Dar, only the pieces of his face were in strange places, the way that dead guy Picasso painted. She signed each with a big "J" at the bottom.

I pretended to mumble the last words of the pledge. But all I could see was Jazz and me sitting out under the huge shade tree by the basketball courts. I'm leaning against the trunk with a piece of grass sticking out of my mouth. She's drawing my face.

"Please take out your Outdoor Ed. folders," said Miss Anders, popping my daydream. That weird sub, Ms. Badu, was our teacher for only one day, but she sure made me appreciate Miss Anders being back. My life was mixed up enough without some strange sub shaking it up.

Miss A gave Maggie permission to get a book out of her locker, then wrote Reptiles and Amphibians on the board. But when Maggie walked back to her desk, Mack whispered something to her. She put her hands on her hips, screwed up her mouth and said, "Just because Dad's out of town doesn't mean you can start up with me again. I mean it, Mack."

"And what're you going to do about it, you little tattletale? Run to the stone statues?"

"Don't talk about Jim and Ryan that way!"

Miss Anders, spun around. "Mack, Maggie?"

"We're fine, Miss Anders," Maggie said, turning to give Mack a mean look. "I just had to ask Mack something about our older brothers." She was about to sit down, but she didn't. She stopped to look at me. Her eyes looked sad. Or was it scared? Then she slid into her seat and put her head down.

I felt bad for her. If I had a sister, I sure wouldn't treat her that way. I leaned forward, tapped her shoulder and said, "Hey Maggie. Don't you just hate it when—"

"We're going to begin a discussion on Florida reptiles and amphibians," said Miss Anders. Does anyone know the difference between the two?"

Before Maggie could reply to my tap, I shot my hand in the air. Miss A looked totally surprised and seriously happy when she called on me. I hadn't exactly been participating much since Dad had left town.

"You can tell an amphibian by its smooth skin," I said. Maggie turned around and I smiled at her, hoping she'd forgotten about her stupid brother. Plus, it gave me something to focus on instead of getting all googlie-eyed at Jazz.

"But snakes and turtles and alligators all have scaly skin, so that makes them reptiles," I added, thinking I was starting to sound just like Dar.

I sat down and looked sideways without moving my head too much in Jazz' direction. She seemed lost in another face she was sketching.

Me, maybe? It could happen.

Chapter 15
To Stop the Blood

When I pushed through the cafeteria door that afternoon, a CPR dummy was lying on one of the tables! I knew we were going to learn basic first-aid for our camping trip, but CPR? How perfect could that be?

My dad had taught me and he used to let me practice on dummies he'd bring home. I knew exactly what to do!

Mr. Taylor, the newest teacher at DIP, stood behind the table. The girls all thought he was cute but he reminded us boys of a mouse. In my opinion, the guy didn't look old enough to be a teacher. He had this pointy nose and the kind of hair that he had to keep pushing off to the side 'cause it kept falling in his eyes.

"Good afternoon, students. I probably shouldn't be telling you this," he said, smiling at Miss Anders, "but not only is this my first year teaching, this is my first time teaching first aid. I know you'll help by paying close attention."

Something dropped to the floor and Mr. Taylor scrambled to get whatever it was. When he stood back up, he was holding little white cards. I could've been wrong but his hands looked shaky as he shuffled through them. "Just give me a sec," he said, moving the first card to the back, then the second. "Wait. . ." He spun around and I couldn't see what he was doing.

When he turned back, he said, "Sorry about that. Lost my place. Let's—"

"When was the last time you saw it?" yelled Mack, from about five rows of cafeteria seats back.

Scrawny Ned laughed.

"Mr. Malone!" Miss Anders glared at Mack. "That's your first and last warning."

Mr. Taylor took a deep breath. "Let's begin. First things first. No matter what kind of injury occurs, find an adult to help." Then he took his cell phone out of his shirt pocket and pointed to it. "If an adult isn't available, call 911."

Maggie raised her hand. Mr. Taylor looked at his cards again, moved another one to the back, and then nodded for her to speak.

"What do we do if we don't have a phone and only kids are around?"

"That would be a good question. And it's in my lecture. Please. I'd appreciate it if you would hold your questions for now and not interrupt me. But, in that situation you do the best you can do, and I will tell you what to try."

"Do we get a weal diploma?" Ned sounded serious.

83

Mr. Taylor rolled his eyes. "No, Ned. You will not get a diploma. This is an overview. Someday, take a real first aid course."

"Your most likely problem in the woods will be mosquitoes, spiders, wasps, Bumble bees, and fire ants. So we'll talk about that first. Usually, bug bites won't be a big deal. If it's a bee or wasp, just scrape off the stinger, clean it thoroughly, put some ice on it and then some first aid cream. But if a spider bites you, it's important to get a good look at it."

Mr. Taylor held up pictures of spiders and ID'd each. The black widow had a red spot on its back that looked like an hourglass. The brown widow's spot was the same shape but yellow.

"Excellent photographs," Dar said, straining to get a closer look. "Must have used a macro lens."

Jazz cringed and stuck out her tongue. "I hate spiders. Ach!"

I thought, don't worry about spiders, Jazz. I'll keep them away from you—if you'll let me.

One kid whistled.

"Take a close look at these," Mr. Taylor said. "If you're bitten by a widow spider and no adult is available, tie something just above the bite. Tight, but not tight enough to stop blood from circulating. This is important. I repeat. Tight, but not tight enough to stop the blood from circulating. That will prevent most of the venom from moving. Then put a cold compress on it, get help, and get to a hospital."

Over the next hour, Mr. Taylor showed us how to take care of minor cuts, burns, blisters and splinters. He passed out bags full of first aid supplies and we were supposed to treat ourselves for different injuries: a bug bite, a splinter, a burn, a cut.

It was so cool, cleaning fake bites, cutting bandages and stuff. Otie and another kid didn't know how to dress a wound, so I helped them. Then I moved on to help a few other kids. Any luck, Jazz might be paying attention and want some help.

Miss Anders excused herself, saying she'd be back shortly. As soon as the cafeteria door closed, Mack and Ned used long ace bandages to wrap each other like mummies. I have to admit they looked pretty funny. Kids started laughing until Mr. Taylor looked up.

"Students?" His voice was quiet as he scanned the room.

Mack walked toward me, his hands out in front, fingers spread, kind of like Frankenstein.

"Students!" Mr. Taylor's voice got louder. "Mack. Ned. That will be enough! Take off those bandages right now. Class. Please get back to work. CLASS!"

It took him forever to get us quieted down. I swear the guy was actually counting to ten. Then he walked over to a phone on the wall and turned his back to us.

When he finally hung up, he said, "One interruption after another. I have never. . ." and then he started putting some of his supplies back in the containers lined up on the floor. Mack pointed at Mr. Taylor and fake laughed, his mouth open and his body

85

shaking like he was busting a gut, but without any sounds coming out. Then Jazz copied Mack's pretend laugh and for some reason, she looked at me.

It's not like I hadn't ever heard about peer pressure. I knew not to let it get me to do something I didn't think was right. But the pressure at that moment hit me like a bowling ball the size of a huge bolder and I fake laughed, too.

The cafeteria door swung open and slammed against the wall. In strolled Mr. Blowford, who happened to be staring at me mid laugh.

"Mack Malone, Ned Barkley." His voice was scarily calm. "To my office. Spanky McDougal! You can join them."

My body got the shakes and when I looked around, most everyone had frozen saucer eyes. Jazz shrugged. Dar and Maggie stared at the floor.

I'd been such a jerk. I totally deserved to be in trouble. I picked up my stuff and followed Mack and Ned.

"Mr. Blowford," called Mr. Taylor. "May I speak to you a moment?"

Mr. Taylor met him at the door and the two talked while the three of us waited outside in the hallway. Mack was still pretend laughing. At me. Ned had his hands over his mouth, like he might burst at any second. I wanted to kick them both where the sun doesn't shine.

But the only foot action that was going to happen was by Blowfish, when he kicked the three of us out of the camping trip. It hit me that he'd have to call our parents. My stomach got sick. He'd call my mom. She'd get even more depressed. Maybe he'd call the Army to talk to Dad. Oh man, Dad would be so upset with me. He might get distracted from what he should be paying attention to and end up . . .

"Mr. McDougal." I felt a tap on my shoulder.

I spun around and was looking eye to eye with Blowfish. "Mr. Taylor seems to think you have something to contribute in there. I suspect you might, as well. Go back inside, but consider this a warning."

"Yes, Sir!"

As I jammed on the metal bar to open the cafeteria door, I looked back. The three of them were heading to Blowfish's office. But Mack turned and our eyes locked. I wanted to fake laugh at him. But Taylor had saved my butt. No way was I going to take a chance and mess things up.

When I walked in, the room erupted in a buzz. Taylor yelled, "Students. You will settle down, now! You've wasted so much time. I'll never be able to cover everything."

I took my place next to Dar, raised my hand, and said, "Excuse me, Mr. Taylor. What about the dummy?"

He stared at me as if he was deciding whether to answer or smack me. Then he looked around the room. "Who knows something about CPR?"

No one moved. A couple kids quietly said things like, "just a little." I looked over at Dar. He shook his head, no. I shook my head yes, and put up my fist. He rolled his eyes and frowned. Then he smacked my fist with his.

"It's a bump, Dar," I whispered. "Not a punch." We definitely had to work on that!

Chapter 16
Very Afraid

A CPR dummy looks like a kid chopped in half—head, neck, chest—but no arms and no body below the waist. I was feeling a little, well, spunky, knowing something I could show the other kids, especially Jazz. And besides, Mr. Taylor reminded me a little of my mom when she got depressed. He just seemed like he could use a little help.

He looked at me waving my hand, almost like he was daring me to give him a hard time. "Come up here, Spanky."

As I headed up front, Jazz asked permission to get a drink of water. Terrific.

"So Spanky," said Mr. Taylor, in a calmer voice. "Where did you learn CPR?" Then he pulled out a box of plastic gloves.

"At Boy— at summer camp," I said quietly, rubbing Dad's compass in my pocket.

"And what is the first thing you do?" Taylor's voice actually sounded friendly now, almost helping me along.

Before I could answer, the cafeteria door swung open and in came Miss Anders. Taylor nudged me with his arm. "The first thing, Spanky?"

"Call 911 for help. Then put on personal safety equipment. Those gloves for instance. There's also a special covering that goes over the person's mouth if you still plan on doing the mouth-to-mouth part. Some people say you shouldn't go near their mouth."

"Yeah, unless you want to kiss them or something," someone whispered loud enough for everyone to hear.

The class cracked up.

"That will be enough!" said Miss Anders.

It seemed funny to me to worry about germs. I mean if a person's about to die are you really going to stop and put on gloves and a mask? I doubt it. But I guess you have to be careful with all the weird germs around.

"And what do you do next?" asked Taylor.

I pulled on my gloves, slowly, to hold things up till Jazz got back. I put my gloved hand on the dummy's forehead and lifted his chin. Tilting his head back, I pretended to look down his throat, killing more time.

Jazz walked in, so I went into action, for real. "You tilt his head back to open up the airway and check for clogs," I said, lifting his chin, and then finding Jazz in the crowd. "You're also supposed to see if he's breathing."

90

Taylor's voice actually sounded excited when he said, "And if he's breathing, Spanky, do you need to do CPR?"

Brrrrrrring.

I couldn't believe it. Everyone was grabbing their stuff and heading to the cafeteria door. People always say "saved by the bell". But it sure hadn't saved my chance to get Jazz's attention.

Dar and I talked the whole way home, about Scouting, camping, our Outdoor Ed. projects. As for Mack, well, he sat up front right behind Alice again. Seemed like he ended up there every time he got in trouble. Only this time, Ned was sitting next to him.

Mr. Taylor had gotten his revenge.

***

I guess I expected to find Ned and Mack sitting behind Alice the next morning. But that seat was empty and Ned sat way in back. Where was—

Alice must've read my mind. "If you're looking for Mack, don't worry sugar. He's not here today."

When she drove into the school parking lot, there he was, sitting in a parked car with some older man. The guy looked like he was yelling at Mack. With the windows closed, I couldn't be sure.

I told Dar I'd catch up with him, and bent down as if I was looking for something. I waited for the shuffle of shoes to go away. When everyone was off the bus, I looked up. Alice and some teacher were talking in front of school. I was safe.

Back inside the car, the old guy grabbed Mack with both hands. He yanked him close to his face and shook him. Then he shook Mack again, like he was nothing but a rag doll. I could tell Mack was saying something but it was like watching one of those old silent movies. The whole time I watched them I kept pushing and pulling the top of the seat in front of me as if it were me shaking Mack.

The old guy let go with one hand and made a fist with the other. His face was all scrunched up as he yelled at Mack who looked afraid. Very afraid.

I had to get to class, but I couldn't stop staring. That is, until Alice's voice butted in. "Don't think you're going to play hooky on my bus." She was smiling. "You gonna stay here all day?" Better get moving if you don't want to be late."

I ran down the aisle and jumped off the bus steps. About the same time Mack was getting out of the car, I hit the ground.

"Will you stop, already, Daddy?" he yelled. Mack's face was red and I swear he'd been crying. "I heard you. But forget it. I'm not them, so just stop!" Then he slammed the door and bolted. But not before he saw me watching him.

I don't know where he went. He never came to class. I wondered who *them* was. And why didn't he want to be them?

When I got home later, I found an email from Dad waiting for me. I opened it so fast I almost deleted it by mistake. All I can say is that I wish I hadn't read it.

Chapter 17
Big As the Whole Outdoors

A couple mornings later, the phone rang just as I was running out the kitchen door. I circled back to grab the phone. "Hello?" I said, looking up at the clock.

"Spanky? It's Dad!"

"Hey Dad! What's up?" Mom came rushing into the kitchen, eyes swollen, just like the day she'd yelled at me about unpacking.

"I know you've been busy with school," he said, "You never answered my last email. Or did I miss a letter from you?"

Dad was right. That last email, the one I wished I hadn't read said he'd be leaving for Afghanistan in a couple days, on September 27th to be exact. I never answered it. I couldn't answer it. What was I supposed to say?

I looked at the calendar hanging on the fridge door. It was September 27th, all right. I handed Mom the phone and bolted out the door. Inside my head I was yelling, "NO! NO! NO!" but the only thing that came out of me was tears. At the bus stop, Alice pulled around the corner so I hid behind a bush and waited.

She waited.

I didn't know what to do. I didn't want to go to school, but I didn't' want to go home, either. I waited her out.

With the bus out of sight, I took off again, running hard and fast until I couldn't run anymore. I ended up at the Minute Stop with an ache in my side. Dad's compass was pinching my leg. Couldn't catch my breath. Had to lean against a garbage can.

Through the glass door, I saw the candy rack and Dad's favorite Junior Mints. I bent over, held my arm against my rib, and waited for the pain to go away.

I wanted to take off again. To run and never come back.

Instead, I paced back and forth until I could finally breathe again and headed back home. Mom was in the kitchen, staring out the window.

"I'm not feeling so good," I said, and went to the sink for a glass of water.

Mom must not have heard me. I reached around her to fill my glass and then went to my room.

I had to fix things.

Dear Dad:

I'm really, really sorry for not talking to you. I acted like a little kid. You don't have to worry about anything. I promise. Like I told you. You can count on me. Have a good trip. Okay? Write me as soon as you get there.

Spanky

I didn't actually say goodbye, but I could breathe again. He answered almost immediately!

Dear Spanky:
I was just writing YOU a letter! I had a few minutes and I have to tell you, I was a little worried there. But you know what? This saying goodbye business isn't easy. I actually thought of waiting to call you once I settled in overseas. I'd say hello instead of having to say goodbye. Don't worry about it, pal. I know what you're all about. Everything's going to be fine.
The next time I say hello it'll be from Afghanistan. I love you,

Dad

Dad crossed like ten time zones. I couldn't remember if that added a day or took one away. Which made me wonder. If something were to happen to either him or me, could we keep it from happening by flying back in time? Anyway, after you figured out whether he was ten hours ahead or behind, you had to add or subtract some more hours. Every morning, when I was walking to the bus stop, I imagined my dad with a bunch of other soldiers. They'd be walking through the mountains. Or maybe the desert or just heading back to base. On my way home from school, he'd be in his barracks, asleep on a cot.

I'd sent him a couple emails, but for some reason, they bounced. He called Mom's cell phone at her temp jobs. Then at dinner, she'd tell me what he'd said:

"They moved Dad from a big air base in Bagram to a small base just outside Farah. He said to look it up."

"The food over there is okay, but he thinks about my Crock Roast every day."

"They're having problems with their communications center. It'll be fixed in a few days."

Then one night, over leftover meatloaf, Mom's voice got all shaky. "So...Dad wanted me to tell you that he might not always be able to talk about where he's going or what he's doing."

"Why? Is he doing something top secret?" I swallowed a mouthful of meat, imagining Dad in some special unit, sneaking around like a spy.

"No." Mom pushed her plate away. "But they never know who might be listening on their telephones or intercepting emails. It's just a way to keep them safe."

She smiled at me while I ate. She hadn't taken a bite. Her face looked puffy and her chalky skin didn't go with her smile. I didn't want to keep staring at her face so I piled more rice on my plate.

"Dad also said to tell you if he says, 'I won't be able to email for a while,' we shouldn't get worried. He's not going to say where he's going. He can't tell us how long he'll be away. It just means he's on patrol, doing his job."

Sure enough, a few nights later, Mom said, "Dad didn't call me today. I guess he's..." Her voice squeezed shut.

"He's doing his job, Mom. He's doing his job."

"I'm sure you're right, Spanky. It's just that. . ."

"Mom!" I yelled, throwing my hands up in the air. "Think about it. When Dad was home. Did he call you every day from work?"

Her face got a little brighter. "I know you're right. I'm sorry, Spanky. I'm sure you're worried too."

"No I'm not!" I pushed my plate away. "Don't ever say that. Dad's saving people over there. That's why he can't call you."

The heel of mom's shoe was tapping the tile. She picked up her water and ended up knocking it over. Both of us grabbed napkins and were wiping it up, but then she started crying and ran to the kitchen. I found her standing at the sink, staring out the window. "I'm sorry, Mom."

She didn't turn around, but said, "What would I do without you?"

I wondered.

***

When I got off the bus the next afternoon, I walked to the Minute Mart to buy a Snickers bar. When it was time to pay, I dug for some change and ended up pulling out Dad's compass, too. After staring at it, I ran back to the candy row to find some malted milk balls for Mom.

98

She'd made it to work that day and when she got home, I met her at the door. "Dad called, right?"

She shook her head, pushed past me and headed to her room.

I yelled, "He'll call tomorrow." I kept wondering if I should tell Dad about how bad Mom was getting. But if I told him, he'd be all worried about her. He'd only been overseas for a few days. Was it going to be like this every time he wasn't able to get to a phone?

The Snickers felt like a rock in my stomach. Then I heard his voice saying, "I knew I could count on you." Which made me wonder what he would do right about now.

I searched the fridge for something to make for dinner. Ended up fixing a frozen pizza, and stared out the window while I waited. Man did the house feel quiet, like the power had gone out all over again.

Out back, I picked a pink hibiscus and put it in a glass with some water. When I ran back to my room to get the bag of malted milk balls, I heard, "And tonight on Inside Edition—" coming from the living room. Perfect, I thought. Mom was up.

I put a flower, the bag of candy and two plates of pizza on a tray. I found Mom on the couch. So I pulled over a TV table. When I set the tray in front of her, her face changed. It went from blank to, well, weird. Smiling, really smiling. Like I'd somehow magically brought Dad back from Afghanistan. Like it was him who'd set the tray in front of her.

The pizza smelled so good. I wolfed my slice down in a few bites and got sauce all over my fingers.

Mom's face looked even mushier, when she said, "Your heart is as big as the whole outdoors, honey."

"No way." I clenched my hand into a tight ball. "My heart's only as big as my fist. Learned that in fourth-grade science. See?" I put this goofy grin on and stuck my messy fist close to her face.

Mom's mouth puckered up. She jerked backward and a giggle popped out—only a little giggle, but she looked surprised. One slipped out of me. Then she giggled again and pretty soon we were both holding our bellies, laughing like Dad was on his way home from work and we were the happiest family in the world.

It hit me how little things like a flower or malted milk balls seemed to make Mom feel like Dad was back with us or we were with him. And it gave me an idea.

I grabbed an empty box from the garage and set it on the dining room table. Then I ran around the house looking for stuff for Dad.

Little bottles of shampoo. Trail mix. Some samples of wet wipes that came in the mail to help him get the sand off. Tube socks. Can't have too many socks.

None of it was too exciting. But it'd let him know we were always thinking about him. Who knows? Maybe it'd make his life a little easier over there so he could be on his best game.

I had tried to get my mom to help, but she'd already gone to bed.

Chapter 18
Jazz, Jazz, Jazz, Jazz

The next morning, the sound of water spilling over our gutters and splashing into a puddle on the ground woke me up. A perfect day to keep sleeping. Behind my closed eyes . . .

Dad is holding up a bag of trail mix. He waves at me like he wants me to follow him. He walks faster. With each step, I swear he gets taller. He's a giant. The ocean is up ahead. The water meets the sand. It's a cliff. When he reaches it, he stops. He looks back at me. He waves and calls out, "Hello!" Then he turns back to the ocean and slips off the edge—

Click. Beep, beep, beep...beep, beep, beep...beep, beep, beep

I slammed the snooze bar and accidentally knocked Dad's compass off my night table. I'd kept it near me all the time since he'd left. During the day, I liked feeling it in my pocket. In bed, it stared at me from my night table.

I reached down to pick it up. It felt warm in my palm—almost like I could feel Dad's hand. Man, it was a beauty: all brass, had his initials carved into the back.

Mom stopped at my door, looking so tired. Last night's giggles were gone. "I'll give you a lift," she said, "but we need to get going if you want me to mail that box before I go to work."

I set the compass on my desk and as I brushed my teeth, I tried to think positively. So what if Dad was in Afghanistan and I was in Appalacheeville. So what if I couldn't count on my Mom. Nothing was going to change. I just had to get on with things. Like my Outdoor Ed report. And it was about time I talked to Jazz.

I smashed down the cowlick on the back of my head. But it had other ideas.

Dark clouds dumped sheets of rain on us as Mom drove to DIP. It was like driving through a carwash! Passing cars swamped us. And when we drove over puddles, the water splashed up under the car. I could feel it vibrate the floor.

What the heck was I going to say to Jazz? I stared out the blurry window, watching the windshield wipers swish across it. Thump thump. Thump thump. Should I? Should I? Talk to. Talk to. Jazz. Jazz. Jazz. Jazz. What if I tried and she walked away?

The closer we got to school, the harder it rained, the faster the windshield wipers swished, and the faster my foot thumped. I wanted Mom to turn around. Just turn right around and drive home so I could go back to bed.

So much for positive thinking.

"You sure seem in a hurry to get to class," she said.

I shrugged. She totally didn't get it, but then how could she? We didn't talk about me or school for more than a minute every night.

We pulled up at DIP way too early. The parking lot was almost empty. I got out and watched Mom drive away. My legs couldn't decide whether to run into the building or chase after her.

Inside the heavy double-doors, the air hit me like a blast from the ice-cream freezer at the Publix supermarket. The school's air-conditioning could sure turn your sweat into ice water on rainy days.

I jammed my hands in my pants pockets and took the stairs two at a time to warm me up. My fingers immediately noticed the missing compass—I'd forgotten to put it in my pocket! Must have had a bad case of Jazz on the mind.

At the landing, I almost tripped over my shoe lace. I slammed through the set of double doors, expecting to walk into a crowd of kids. But it was way too early. The doors crunched shut behind me. Sounds echoed off the hall walls.

103

"Whoa!" I stopped short. Someone had tacked up new posters to the bulletin boards that hung between each bank of lockers.

GET TO KNOW YOUR FLORIDA TREES
Sleep under them
PREPARE TO ROUGH IT!
Less Than Three Weeks until the Annual Overnight
OUTDOOR ED REPORTS are DUE THIS WEEK
Show What You Know!"

Holy-moly. We really were going camping! I turned the corner to my classroom and found a few kids sitting on the floor right outside the door. They were huddled over secretly texting away on their cell phones. Probably to each other. Pretty lame if you ask me. Even if we could afford a cell phone for me.

I set my backpack on the floor. With my foot propped up on it, I retied my sneaker, but I kept dropping the loop. And what did I see heading toward me through the opening between my knees? Black Army boots.

My butt was staring Mack Malone straight in the face.

"Well, if it isn't Butt-wipe McDougal hiding something again."

I bolted upright but before I could spin around...

"Hiding something just like you did on the—"

. . .Mack's boot and my right butt cheek connected.

"—bus!"

His kick sent me flying forward into a bank of lockers. BAM! My hands had been too busy tying my shoe so nothing stopped me when I crashed. After the stars spinning in my head went away, I spun around to defend myself to counter his kick—a move Dad had shown me a long time ago. But when I stepped forward, my backside felt like it'd been stabbed. I kind of wobbled.

Mack's head snapped left to look down the hall. A group of teachers had just come out of a classroom and were headed our way.

"Don't even think about opening your mouth, McDougal," hissed Mack.

But the teachers ignored us. They seemed to be in a deep discussion. Part of me wanted to grab one of them and plead for help.

The other part of me wanted to get revenge.

Chapter 19
Oxes? Oxen?

Mack had shuffled over to his locker, eyeing the teachers who were heading downstairs when Dar turned the corner to our hallway. "Spank. I could use a hand." Dar was holding his backpack in his arms with his laptop wedged under his chin. His glasses were crooked to the side and about to fall off.

I took off down the hall, knowing the guy couldn't see a thing without them. "Talk about perfect timing," I said, and pushed his frames back up his nose. "Mack got me again." I looked back over my shoulder at Mack who slammed his locker shut.

"I'm listening," Dar said.

"Ok. I was tying my shoe and Mack walks up and kicks me in the, in the. . .what is all of this stuff?" I freed the laptop from his jaw grip. "What are you. . .moving into school?"

"Yes. You've guessed correctly. I've run away from home and am moving into school. Soon I'll join the circus."

"Very funny, Dar."

Mack was heading our way. His beady eyes locked on to us. I didn't want to show fear so I tried to stare him down. But he sprang at us. I mean the guy actually looked like a hungry cougar. He landed within spitting distance, right in front of Dar.

I swear Mack was drooling, like he'd found himself a meaty bone. He kept moving his weight from one foot to the other, as if he might spring again. "Morning, Brain Sluuuudge."

Dar and I tried to ignore him, tried to keep walking. But in two moves, Mack shoved me out of the way, hard, and bumped up against Dar's backpack with his chest.

"Well now, brain-boy, what's your rush?" he said, blocking Dar and then bumping against him again. "I reckon you want to impress your sweetie pie, Miss Anders. Probably want to make kissy face with her, now isn't that right?"

Dar tried to dodge him, but Mack pulled at the side of Dar's backpack. "Brain Sluuudge," he drawled. "Look at all those library books." Then in a squeakier voice, "Oh Miss Anders. Ain't I just the smartest brownnoser in the class?"

Suddenly it seemed like the whole school showed up. Kids circled us, looking like a bunch of buzzards. I was about to force myself between Mack and Dar, the way our teachers do to break up a fight, but Dar backed away.

Mack lunged forward and grabbed hold of his backpack. "Let me help you with that. This here's too heavy for a skinny straw like you."

Okay, so Dar wasn't that meaty. But he pulled back hard, only Mack held firm. Dar twisted and Mack tugged and the backpack flew out of Dar's hands, scattering books in every direction, like an explosion.

Mack shook his head. "Brain Sluuuudge. Now why'd you want to go and throw your books all over the floor?"

It didn't seem right, him giving Dar a bad time. He seemed to divvy up his abuse between the two of us and it was actually my day. I held on to Dar's laptop while he leaned over to scoop up his books. But Mack shoved his boot between Dar's shoes. Splat. Dar went down, taking me with him.

Luckily, I managed to save the laptop. But my butt had hit the floor right where Mack had kicked me. Oh man, that hurt bad. I couldn't move. And Mack's boots were planted right beside me.

The other kids stared at Dar, who by that point was lying face down. Then Jazz pushed through the crowd. Her eyes shouted He's your friend. Do something! It was my chance. Not only could I help my friend, I'd impress Jazz, and have something cool to tell my dad!

I slid Dar's laptop toward him and tried to get up. But Mack slammed me down again, hard. Ok, maybe I was off balance, but that guy was as strong as an ox. Maybe ten oxes . . .oxen . . .or whatever they're called. At that point, both my butt and my shoulder hurt.

"Look at your little pal, McFrugal," Mack said, sneering at me. "The brainiac's got two left feet to match his four eyes! Come on, Butt-wipe. Aren't you gonna help your little buddy?"

In my head, I imagined swinging Mack by his ankles and throwing him through the air into the lockers. But in real life, my legs were acting like I was in a nightmare, the kind where something scary is chasing after you and you want to run but your legs feel like wet spaghetti.

My jaw hurt from gritting my teeth. My hands curled into fists, but I just sat there where Mack had slammed me, frozen.

Dar lay splattered next to me; must've tasted the janitor's clean floor, all piney and moppy smelling. And there I sat, my stomach wanting to upchuck my breakfast, and my brain wondering why I couldn't move.

Sweeping the tile with his arms, Dar said, "Glasses. Where are my glasses?"

The frames had gone one way and the lenses another. I managed to pick up his lenses and hand them to him. Then I used my sneaker to push the frames across the floor, to where Dar's windshield wiper arms could find them.

I whispered, "Over here, Dar."

"Watch yourself, you little carrot-topped dweeb," said Mack, who seemed more interested in something down the hall, "or I'll kick you again."

The clicking sound of Miss Anders' heels echoed off the DIP green lockers. She'd turned the corner to our hall and Mack took off in the other direction. Dar had sat up and was holding his frames in one hand and his lenses in the other, squinting.

"Let me help you with those," I said, wanting to put his lenses back in his frames, but Jazz beat me to the punch.

She said, "You okay? Give them to me, Dar." Then she kneeled down. Dar looked toward her voice. Then he turned toward me as he handed the lenses and frames to Jazz.

"What's happened here?" asked Miss Anders.

The pain in my butt and shoulder yelled, "Don't say a word. Keep your mouth shut!"

Before I could argue with myself, Jazz spoke up. "Mack tripped Dar. Twice. And his glasses flew off. And now they're broken!"

Great. Jazz stood up for Dar. Never mentioned what Mack did to me. Probably didn't even know I was alive.

"All of you go inside and sit down," Miss Anders said.

I got up and held out a hand to Dar. He ignored it or maybe he couldn't see it. I bent down to help him, but he said, "I can manage, thank you." I couldn't tell whether he was embarrassed or mad or both, probably.

I shoved my hands into my pockets, reminding me Dad's compass was still on my night table at home. I managed to limp into class where Miss Anders was standing next to the wall, talking on the school phone. A short while later, the bell rang and Maggie walked through the door. At least someone hadn't seen me wimp out. But on her way to her desk, she looked at me again—this time, square in the eyes.

If Mack's eyes were cold and hard, hers were more like, I don't know. . .maybe pillows? Something about them, the way she looked at me, made me think she got how much I hated her brother.

"Psst." Jazz tried to get Maggie's attention, and passed her a note.

I watched Maggie read it, dying to know what Jazz wrote. Maggie folded the note back up and then looked over at. . . well, I wasn't sure, but I thought she was looking at Dar. I followed her stare, which moved from Dar back to Jazz. The two of them smiled and I swear Jazz was blushing.

What was that all about?

After the pledge and announcements, I asked Miss Anders if I could be excused. I stumbled to the boys' bathroom. Inside, I leaned against the sink and stared at my reflection.

So much for making you proud, Dad. Did you like how I saved my best friend? And how about how I stood up to a bully?

My turn to be the hero?

Yeah, right.

Chapter 20
"M" Words

When I got back from the bathroom, Miss Anders was hanging up the school phone a second time. There was a quiet buzz, like kids were wondering what was going to happen.

Miss A didn't turn around right away. It was weird. She just stood there for a while, resting her forehead on the wall. When she finally faced us, her skin looked a little pale, like maybe she was coming down with something. Then she said, "Mr. Malone. Please pack up your books. Mr. Blowford wants to see you in his office immediately. And I suggest you take everything you'll need to work on for tomorrow."

"What? Oh, great." Mack pulled a couple books out from under his desk and slammed them on top. Then he spun around to me and whispered over Maggie, "I'm taking myself a little vacation, Cub Scout. But when I get back, you're next." Then he got up and took his good-ole sweet time, his army boots shuffling up our aisle and out the door.

I had a clear view without the back of Mack's head in my way and I could breathe easy. Wally the Weather Guy would've needed a bunch of M words to predict how I was feeling about Mack being gone. Meteoric. Magnificent. Marvelous. Yeah, Mack-free.

When the lunch bell rang, I caught up to Dar. "Wanta eat outside or are you doing the "Eating with Einstein" thing?"

"Sorry. Simultaneous *Chess* and *Go* tournaments today."

"Oh. Okay. Well, see ya." I headed outside to a nice patch of grass under the big Oak tree by the basketball court.

When I slid down the trunk to the ground, my butt still hurt from being kicked. But my stomach was growling like a hungry dog. I ripped the wrap off my meatball sandwich. With each bite, I imagined the scene back in the hall with Mack. It went a lot different that time, that's for sure. And it wasn't Dar who Jazz was acting all nice to.

"Spanky?"

The sound of grass crunching and Dar's voice brought me back to reality.

"Are you out here?" he called.

What happened to his tournaments? "Over here!"

Dar fast walked up to me, his arms pumping with each step—he hated to run. "Coming!" When he got close, he shoved his fist next to my mouth.

113

It took me a second to figure out what he was doing, but when I did, and put my fist out, he smacked in hard. Again. "We need to work on that," I said, rubbing my hand. "You don't need to break my knuckles every time."

Dar knelt down and was picking blades of grass. Probably examining an insect or taking global warming readings or something. But then he stood up again and walked in a circle, mumbling. First he said, "Yeah . . . maybe humor." Then he shook his head like he didn't like the idea.

I cupped my palm to shade my eyes from the sun, looking up to him. "Maybe humor what?"

"Talking to myself," he said and knelt back down. "And anyway, the direct approach is always better. So, about your dad."

"My dad?" I still hadn't told him he was in Afghanistan. I hadn't told anyone. "What about him?"

"Look. There's no easy way to say this. Miss A just told me where he is. And thanks, by the way. Why didn't you tell me? What's the big secret?"

I shrugged, but I could tell it really mattered to him. I should've told him. But he never asked. And anyway, I had to think about my dad being gone all the time at home. Why should I have to talk about it at school?

His eyes looked, well, sad maybe when he said, "Miss A's a little worried about you."

"Worried about me? That's crazy. Okay, it's true. My dad's in Afghanistan, but he's fine and I'm fine and

114

my Mom's—." I picked up a stone and sailed it over the basketball court. "My Mom's—"

My brain started spitting truths at me. Your mom is a mess, you want to tell Dad about her, but if you do, it might worry him. And you said you'd handle things even if she is getting worse.

"You were saying about your mom?"

Why didn't anyone get that I didn't want to talk about it. "So how's Scouts?" I asked. "Your troop doing anything cool? And what happened to your Go game?"

"Scouts?" Dar rolled his eyes. "Go game? Spanky! I'm trying to talk to you about your— oh never mind." He opened his little cooler and took out a container of mixed nuts, an apple, a cheese stick, and a carton of Green Tea. No wonder the guy was so skinny.

After a swig of his tea, he said, "Mr. Palumbo cancelled. Had a migraine and wanted to darken the room. So he kicked us out. This is a lovely spot you've found out here."

"Lovely?" I laughed. Only Dar could get away with that. "So, about what happened earlier with Mack."

Dar swallowed a bite of his apple, and said, "Yes, that was unfortunate."

"Unfortunate?" I couldn't believe my ears. Didn't anything upset this guy? "Well, here's the thing. I really wanted to help you. But the truth is..."

I had no clue what the truth was.

Like he was nudging me, Dar repeated, "The truth is . . ."

115

A zillion things flew through my brain. Boxes piled up in my mom's room. Dad running back to me at the airport. Eating by myself when the power went out. Mom not eating and sleeping all the time. Not one single thing that had to do with school or helping Dar.

"The truth is . . ."

Dar rolled his eyes again. "The truth is what? It's so exasperating when people don't finish their sentences. What is the truth?"

I suddenly wanted to take off running. Or slug him. Slug everyone. His words blew a cork inside of me.

"The truth is I went numb or something. Okay? Do you get that? I don't know why. I wimped out. Couldn't move a finger. There. Are you satisfied? And if you want to know, this doesn't usually happen to me. But you wouldn't know that. Okay? So that's my finished sentence."

Dar raised one eyebrow but kept his mouth shut.

I stuffed the rest of my sandwich back in the bag. "I'm out of here."

Dar spun around on the ground. "May I ask where you're going?"

"To the library to work on my Outdoor Ed report," I said, and started to run in the direction of the building. But then everything in my life would have been totally screwed up.

I stopped and turned around to face Dar. "I'm sorry, okay?"

Dar just nodded.

In the corner of the library, I found an empty table as far away from the librarian's counter as I could get. I opened my notebook to a clean page. Clicked my pen. Got up and searched the library for any new books on snakes. Found two and brought them back to my seat: A Field Guide to Florida Snakes, and The Outdoor Book of Florida Snakes.

I opened the first one and flipped through it. I opened the second one and flipped through it. Then for the next fifteen minutes, I flipped back and forth between wondering why I had wimped out that morning and why I had just yelled at Dar.

Word on the bus that afternoon was that Mr. Blowford gave Mack a two-day suspension. I smiled the whole way home. For 48 hours, nothing was going to bother me.

Chapter 21
Snakelike Green Beans

I found my box of camping gear in the garage after school. My hiking shoes, canteen, even my backpack all had that smoky, campfire kind of smell. I closed my eyes and breathed it in. I couldn't believe how strong the smell was. Too strong. Way too—

I ran inside. Even before I got to the kitchen, I saw smoke.

"MOM! FIRE!" I yelled, but she didn't move. A towel on the stove top was smoldering.

"Water!" Mom cried, looking around the room. "There!"

I grabbed the pot on the counter she'd pointed to and poured it over the towel. Uncooked rice and water poured on the stove, down the side and onto the floor. I ran back to the sink, refilled the pot and dumped it on too.

We stared at the stove, at the floor covered with rice in puddles of water, at the smoke that still hung in the air.

"I must have put the towel on the stove instead of the rice," Mom said. She rubbed her hands. They were shaking. "Thank goodness it was wet."

Really? I couldn't believe what she'd just said. Thank goodness it was wet? I mean what if it hadn't been? What if I hadn't smelled the smoke? "Mom, why did you—, I mean why didn't you—"

"I . . . I . . . I made a mistake. That's all. Help me clean up this mess. And promise me you won't tell Dad about this. He has enough to worry about."

As I mopped up the mess, I wanted to yell, is this what life is going to be like with Dad gone. After my morning with Mack and flipping out on Dar at lunch, now this?

Man did I miss my dad. He and I would have talked about Mack and how to handle him. Or why I froze. Would Mom even understand? It didn't' matter. She was miles away. More like an ocean of miles.

She couldn't stop shaking. That was something new. But I guess we'd never had a fire at the house.

I told her to sit down and tell me how to fix the rice and stuff. At dinner, I moved my green beans snakelike into a long row across the middle of my plate. Then I packed my rice into what looked like a long sand dune to hold up the row of green beans.

"Spanky!" Mom snapped. "Stop playing with your food."

I about jumped out of my seat. Mom never yelled at me for that. She once said there was an artist in me that needed to "express himself" or something crazy like that. But her eyes were all blazing.

"Okay...okay, Mom." I shoveled rice into my mouth, almost choking on it.

She put her fork down, got up from the table, and went into the kitchen. When she came back, she was wiping her eyes with a tissue. "I'm sorry, honey. I'm. . .I'm not mad at you." Then she started sobbing. "I'm mad at just about everything else, but I sure took it out on you."

I wasn't listening to her anymore. A light bulb had just gone off in my head. The same exact thing had happened to me when I yelled at Dar. I wasn't mad at him. Mack, maybe. Myself, definitely. The Army totally. But not Dar.

I guess I'd been staring at my lap, 'cause when I looked up to tell her I knew exactly what she meant, she was gone. I ran to my room to make sure Dad's compass was still on my desk where I'd left it that morning.

Two days passed without Mack. My 48-hour vacation would be over the next morning.

Chapter 22
A Painful Looking Yawn

"Which one of you losers squealed? Was it you?"

I creeped up to the wall, peeked and saw Mack pointing his finger in Jazz's face. She had her hands on her hips and the way she held her head, she looked angrier than a cobra getting ready to strike. I flew around the corner ready to . . . I have no clue what I was going to do. But Mack had already moved on.

He pushed Otie against the lockers. "Tell me what you know, Otie." Otie closed his eyes as if he was expecting Mack to punch him.

"Mack Malone? Let him be!"

Miss Anders! I couldn't believe it. Twice in one week. It was almost like he wanted Miss Anders to catch him.

"Don't you move," she yelled. Her wavy black hair whipped behind her as she raced down the hallway. I swear she looked like a movie star or a superhero. Maybe Wonder Woman or something. But by the time she reached us, her face was beet red and she was panting like a dog.

"Mack Malone, I've had just about enough—" She sucked in air like she couldn't breathe.

"—had about enough of you. Do . . . you hear me?" Her forehead got all wrinkly and her eyes looked strange, almost like she'd just gotten slugged or stabbed.

"I didn't do anything, Miss Anders. See—"

"I don't want to hear another word out of you. Your father . . .your father will hear about this!" Miss Anders definitely wasn't breathing very well. "Why can't you . . .can't you behave like Maggie . . . or your brothers?"

Mack blurted out, "I'm not them!" He kicked the ground and then said, "You don't have to tell my dad. Ah, come on, Miss Anders. It wasn't my fault."

Miss Anders squinted, then fired back, "Don't even think about...making excuses, Mack."

The color of her face had changed from red to gray and her eyes were bulging.

"I saw...whole thing," she said. "DO YOU. . . HEAR ME? I SAW THE WHOLE. . ."

Miss A's mouth opened like a yawn, but a painful-looking yawn. She pressed her fist to her chest, letting go of her books and purse. Then she fell sideways, against me. I couldn't hold her and fell into some other kids who fell onto some other kids. We landed in a pile on the floor like a bunch of dominoes.

"Get . . . Mr. . . . Blow—" were Miss Anders' last words before she passed out.

My fingers had snagged strands of Miss A's hair. I wanted to yank them away but I was afraid to move. All of us kids in the pile just sort of stared wild-eyed at each other. Someone yelled, "What's wrong with Miss Anders?" And then it hit us.

"Oh. My. God. Oh my God!"

"Call 911!"

Dar yelled, "Get the CPR kit."

"Someone get the nurse."

"Where is it?"

"Is she dead?"

"Go get Blowfish!"

A couple of kids pulled themselves out of the pile and took off to find him. One girl started crying.

It was all beginning to compute. My teacher was on the floor, maybe dead!

"Spanky. I can't see," Dar yelled. Across the pile, Dar sat up and his glasses were gone again. "Check for respiration! Put your hand near her mouth. See if you feel anything."

I eased my hand out of her hair and stretched it toward her mouth. I didn't feel anything.

Dar yelled, "Is she breathing?"

"No! She needs CPR." My heart hammered as I scrambled on all fours. "Move out of the way. Move!" I kneeled next to Miss Anders'. Her face was so gray. She actually looked like a movie star—a dead one.

The only mouth-to-mouth I'd ever done was with rubber dummies. Pink lipstick. Flowery smell. Miss Anders was definitely no dummy.

"We don't have time for safety gear. Proceed, Spank!" yelled Dar.

"Okay, okay!" I remembered the steps...Left hand on forehead. Lift her chin. Tilt her head back. Lean down. Check for breath on my cheek. Nothing. Pull jaw down. Check for clogs in her throat. Nothing. Oh my God. Nothing!

Her molars stared at me and my thoughts started spinning out of control. Am I really supposed to put my mouth on her mouth? What if I screw up? What if I slip her some spit? Oh my gosh! What if I throw up?

I fumbled with the button under Miss A's chin. Oh jeez. I was unbuttoning my teacher's shirt. In front of the whole class! But I had to, to help her breathe easier.

When I tilted her head back again to open her airway, Jazz screamed, "She's dying, Spanky. Save her, Spanky! Save her!"

"Now, Spanky," Dar yelled.

I wanted to bend forward, to breathe air into her lungs. But instead, it was like I was on top of the lockers, looking down at myself. Not moving.

In my head, I yelled, DO IT, Spanky. Save her! Breathe for her. But I might as well have been asleep in another nightmare. Instead of spaghetti legs, my body was frozen in place.

I couldn't move. Again.

Chapter 23
Take Me Out to the Ballgame

"One, and two, and three, and . . ."

It seemed like I was still up on top of the lockers, looking down, watching Dar give her chest compressions.

Jazz screamed, "She's dying, Spanky. I thought you knew what to do!" Her voice jolted me. Dar was kneeling at Miss A's other side. He had pressed one palm two fingers below the notch in her chest, right below . . . her. . .um. . .her chest. His other palm pressed down on top of the first, and with his fingers locked, he was pumping hard to keep her heart beating.

Dar spit out, ". . . thirteen, and fourteen, and, NOW Spanky. Breathe for her!"

I bent over and covered her mouth with mine. Just as I was about to breathe, I felt a tug on my shoulder.

"Out of the way, gentlemen. Let Nurse Esther take over. Move!"

Blowfish pulled me up. Dar ignored him and felt for Miss A's jaw. He pulled it down and blew two long breaths in her mouth. Miss A gasped.

Ms. Esther pushed me aside and knelt down. She put her ear over Miss A's mouth, I guess to see if she was still breathing. "You're going to be okay, Tammy," she said, smiling. "Stay with me. Do you hear me? Stay with me. You're going to be okay."

Tammy? Miss A's name is Tammy? I'd forgotten teachers had first names. Tam-meee Anders. Whoa.

Mr. Blowford put his arm around my shoulder, which was shaking like a phone on vibrate, and said, "That was quick thinking, Mr. Garfunkle." Then he turned back to the crowd. "Students, everything is under control. An ambulance is on the way. Go to your classrooms immediately and take your seats. Now MOVE!"

Mack passed me, cupping his hand around my ear and whispered, "Nice work, butt-face. Way to fall asleep on the job, you weenie."

I jerked his hand away just as Blowfish said, "You're Shamus Mr. McDougal, the new boy."

"Sp-sp-spanky, sir." My teeth wouldn't stop chattering. I shoved my hands in my pockets to keep them from shaking, but Dad's compass reminded me what a failure I'd been.

"Mr. Garfunkle, why don't you and Mr. McDougal take a few minutes for yourselves? Your guidance counselor will be here any minute to talk to you. Well done, lads."

126

Dar kind of patted my back. "Spank, your neurons are in overdrive. I can't believe how hard you are shaking."

I pulled him farther down the hall, wondering if whatever was going on with my mom was catching. "Very f-funny. I'm use-use-useless. I f-froze. Again."

Dar held me by the shoulders. "I don't agree. We saved her life."

"No...you s-saved her life." I leaned against a locker, trying to chill out. "If-if you hadn't been there to help me, Miss Anders might have—"

The words stuck in my throat. There was no getting around it. I, Spanky McDougal, did nothing to save her life. I did nothing to help Dar when he lay splattered on the floor. Or to help Otie when Mack had him up against the lockers. What difference did it make if I wanted to help all of them? What difference did it make if I had a big heart like Mom said?

Yeah that was me. Spanky McDougal. Big heart, no bark, and definitely no action.

An ambulance siren blared. Kids kept chattering. The footsteps of Emergency Medical Techs rushed up the stairs. I swear I felt like a ball inside an old pinball machine, getting wacked.

Our counselor, Mrs. Huntley, showed up. After whispering back and forth with Blowfish, she moved over to Dar and me and took a hold of our hands.

"How are you boys? That must have been terribly frightening. Spanky, do you want to sit down?" She had to have felt my shakes.

"Nah. I-I-I'll be okay," I said.

Mrs. Huntley gave my hand a squeeze. "Don't worry, boys. The EMTs will take good care of her. So, when did you learn CPR?"

"Last s-summer. Camp," I said through shivering teeth. "But Dar s-saved—"

"Spanky initiated CPR," Dar said. "I took over."

Before I could argue, Mrs. Huntley headed to our classroom to instruct the rest of the kids to walk with us to the cafeteria. When we got there, she made an announcement.

"Students, please be patient. The cafeteria staff is putting out some snacks for you. I'm sure all of this...what you've just experienced...Miss Anders...well, I'm certain it must be upsetting to some of you and—"

The music to "Take Me Out to the Ball Game" interrupted her speech. "Excuse me for just a moment," she said, and pulled out her cell phone.

Everyone got quiet for a second. Then the chattering started all over again. My mind joined in. Upsetting? Of course I'm upset. Heck I totally caved. Again! And now Miss A will probably die, and it will be all my fault, and the kids will—

"Quiet students." Mrs. Huntley slapped her cell shut. "I have some news. Students. Quiet, please!" She waited until all the talking stopped. "The paramedics are taking Miss Anders to the ambulance this very minute. They'll go straight to County General. That's all we know for now."

Mrs. Huntley looked at me and my eyes flooded. I hid them with my palms and bent my head down.

"We've requested the county send over a few crisis counselors," she says. "I hope you'll take this opportunity to talk to them."

I smelled a mixture of left-over cinnamon rolls and asparagus or whatever it was they were cooking for lunch. Thought I might barf. I grabbed a carton of juice and picked a table away from the crowd. At the other end of the room, I turned my chair around away from the room to look out the cafeteria windows.

In the reflection on the glass, a mug shot of me stared back

PART II

Chapter 24
SHUT UP!

So here I sit, staring at myself, remembering how I ended up where I am, wondering how two months went by that fast. Outside the cafeteria window, the basketball courts are still empty. And the blinding sun keeps demanding answers. "Why did you freeze, McDougal? How do you expect to make your dad proud?"

My head hurts from all the sounds drilling into my brain: Chairs clanging, kids buzzing, someone crying. Worse yet, Jazz's words keep playing over and over in my head. *"She's going to die, Spanky! I thought you knew what to do."*

It's raining so hard, those poor *Fat Guys and a Van* movers are totally soaked. At least it's drowning out all the chattering. I take a swig of juice just as the ambulance screeches away, jolting me. Now juice is trickling down the front of my tee shirt. I turn around for a napkin to find Dar staring at me from across the table.

Jazz and Maggie are sitting on either side of him. And Jazz is touching Dar's arm.

"You are seriously courageous, Dar," she says.

My stomach knots. As much as I wish she would say that to me, Dar deserves it. Oh great. She's patting his hand.

"Dar," she adds, "I don't know when I've seen someone in a situation like that act so calmly."

Maggie hands me a napkin and rolls her eyes. "Um, Jazz, have you ever been in a situation like that before?"

"Okay, maybe not."

Maggie says, "That had to have been pretty darn scary, Spanky."

"Thanks." I try to blot the juice, but the stain won't go away. "Dar saved her life. I didn't do anything. End of story."

It seems so strange. Up until this morning, no one besides Dar has had anything to do with me. I totally screw up twice and two girls are sitting at my table. I definitely have no clue how to figure out women.

Sheesh. Get real, McDougal, I tell myself. They're here because Dar is.

Everyone at our table is quiet but all the jabbering going on around us sounds like it is coming through a megaphone:

"I wonder who our sub will be."

"Do you think it'll be that Badoo doo lady again?"

"What if Miss A has a relapse and dies? Will we get another teacher?"

"Man, if Dar hadn't...

I want to scream, SHUT UP! It's driving me nuts. What good does it do to go over every detail again and again? Not that I can get my own thoughts to calm down. I mean, really. Will they tell us if Miss A's okay? Darn it, I knew what to do. It'll be my fault if she doesn't make it. I did set her up for Dar, though. That should count for something. Forget it, McDougal. You froze.

Mack's laughter adds to my brain stew. He and Ned are sitting at a table behind us. "Aren't we the luckiest class in the whole school," he says, punching Ned. "No more teacher. No more books."

Makes me want to barf—all over him.

Suddenly, Mack is standing behind Dar, poking him in the back. "Just like I told you the other day, Brain Sludge. I knew you wanted to make kissy-face with Miss Anders. Lucky you, Spanky couldn't beat you to it." He stares at me and rubs his chin. "Come to think of it, that reminds me of a song. Spanky and Miss Anders sitting in a tree, K-I-S-S-I-N-G."

My brain feels like it's going to burst out of my head. In a flash, I'm out of my seat, spinning around to face him.

"Whoa, Cub Scout. Look who's gotten all fired up." Mack has that crazy look in his eyes as he pushes up his sleeves. "Come on, weenie. Show me what you got."

I clench my fists and move toward him, but our P.E. Coach's face is suddenly right in mine. "Tough morning, kid. Kind of shakes you up." He looks me right in the eyes, sounding kind of sad. "Ya'll have faith in

133

those doctors. They'll have Miss Anders good as new in no time."

Coach Tony turns around to face Mack. In a normal coach voice, he says, "For now, I think what we all need is some fresh air. If you want to speak to the counselors, sit tight. The rest of you, line up. Let's go outside and play some kickball!"

I might have nailed Mack. Ok, maybe I'll never know. I jam the bar down on the cafeteria door and take off running across the field.

But I could've nailed him.

We play some kickball. Sit around talking. Play more kickball. Coach Tony keeps us busy until lunch. After that, we split up for elective classes, like Art and stuff. Classes where we won't need a sub.

***

After school, Dar says he plans to stay late to finish his Outdoor Ed report. They're due tomorrow and Miss A's sub might see it on a schedule. He says his mom could drive me home if I wanted to stay too. I do.

So we head to the library and find a table. Dar fiddles with something in his backpack, and says, "About this morning and Miss Anders—"

About this morning? The morning I froze and almost killed her? I look up from my paper. "Can we just forget about this morning?"

"Forget? That's highly unlikely. I read in one of my dad's magazines that our brains are more apt to store highly charged events forever—"

"Shut up, Dar. Please? Will you just shut up? I'd rather not talk about it. Okay?" I hold my breath, waiting to see if he'll drop the subject.

"Sorry, Spank. We don't have to discuss it if you don't want to."

He keeps his word.

When Mrs. Garfunkle pulls up to drive us home, she's older than I expect. She's in a green electric car. With Dar for a son, what else could she drive?

Dar looks exactly like her. Only her hair is mostly all white. Even the same round wire glasses. "You must be Darwin's new friend, Spanky."

Darwin. Seriously. Darwin? And I'm worried about my name?

She pulls away from the curb about as fast as a turtle. "Darwin, dear, you won't believe what Lame and Able did in the lab today!"

She blabs on about her research rats. Meanwhile, I'm rating her driving from the back seat. If a car in the next lane passes us—minus one.

A minus score means that my life is going to get screwier and I should just stay in bed tomorrow and not go to school.

But if Mrs. Garfunkle's car passes someone, it means everything will miraculously change—plus one.

So far, Mrs. Garfunkle has -24 points. I can already feel the covers over my head, if I ever get home that is.

Dar tells Mrs. Garfunkle about Miss Anders and, the whole time, she keeps taking quick peaks at me in the rear view window. "You and Darwin are such brave young men, Spanky."

"Yes, ma'am, thank you." I want to be polite, so I say, "But Darwin really saved the day," and go back to counting cars. Out of the corner of my eye, I see Dar put his finger to his lips and Mrs. Garfunkle immediately asks him about his Outdoor Ed project. They don't stop talking the rest of the way home.

I don't think Mom and I have ever talked about anything for that long. Since Dad's left, we've barely talked at all. And it's getting worse.

When I walk through the front door, the house is spotless and my favorite smells bombard me. Spaghetti, meatballs, and garlic bread. Mom is cooking. And she's singing, "Don't worry. Be happy. Cause every little thing is going to be all right."

I'm twirling a noodle around my fork when she sets the garlic bread on the table, and sits down across from me. "So did you make any progress on your paper?"

She doesn't look tired anymore. But you never know with my mom. It's like she's on a trampoline, the way her moods bounce up and down. I tell her about working in the library, all the while, trying to pick up a meatball.

Then she says, "I can't keep the surprise. Dad's unit made it back to base today!"

The meatball ends up on the floor. "You heard from him?"

"Yes! He called me at work before he went to sleep. He couldn't tell me much except that he was AOK and misses you. He wanted to surprise you with an email and he wants to hear all about school."

I stare at the meatball on the floor. I should be so happy. But my stomach knots up again. "Hold that thought." I point to the floor, try to make a goofy face and get down on my knees with my back to her. For the third time today, I can't hold back the water works.

I pick up the pieces of meatball off the carpet with one hand and wipe my eyes with the other. How am I going to tell Dad about school? I wipe my face with the bottom of my tee shirt and get up. With a forced smile, I head to the kitchen to dump the meat in the garbage and get a wet rag. After wiping up the mess, I tell Mom all about my great day at school, even about what happened to Miss A. How my new best friend, Darwin, single-handedly saved the day and that I was pretty lucky to have a friend like him.

"Let's pray she recovers soon," Mom says. "Were you frightened seeing all of this happen right in front of you?"

"Nah...well, okay, maybe a little. But I'm fine, Mom. Seriously."

After dinner, she takes her dishes into the kitchen. "How about some ice cream for dessert?"

137

I shrug her off. "Maybe later. Dinner filled me up. Anyway, it's garbage night." I get up from the table to help her. "I've got some homework, too. And I want to look at my report one more time. We should do the dishes if I'm going to get it all done."

"Tell you what. I'll take care of KP duty tonight. You've got enough on your plate. But check your email. I'm sure there's a message from Dad. He's going to want to hear all about what happened today!"

"Yep," I say, turning away from her. "I'm sure he will."

Chapter 25
Mr. Powerful

My computer takes forever to boot up. Who knows? Maybe Dad is picking up the phone to call me for the first time. So I do the math. I subtract two and a half hours from 6:45 pm and change it from p.m. to a.m. So that makes it 4:15 a.m. over there. Nope. It's not going to happen. He's gotta be sound asleep.

I swivel around in my chair. End up facing my bed and the picture of me and Dad on my night table. Beechwood Fire Station's Father-Son day. Dad is standing next to his fire engine, dressed in his fire-fighting uniform, helmet and all. I remember him telling me his uniform weighed over 100 pounds. Even with all that weight on him, he lifted me up with one arm so I could climb in the cab.

I pull Dad's compass out of my pocket and rub it. When I turn back to my computer, sure enough, there's an email from him in my inbox. For a second, I swear I hear the little envelope say, "I heard you froze. Way to make me proud, son."

"Terrific. I throw my hands up in the air, hitting my desk lamp. The shade tilts; the bulb blinds me.

Dad's email says:

Hey Pal!

Sorry about that communication glitch. We (the team I'm in charge of and another team) were out on patrol, like I told you. When we got back, we had no internet or phone connection for a couple days. And get this. There are only two computers for us to use.

It's over 110 degrees in the shade, but you know me. I guess I can handle the heat easier than some of the others.

I laugh out loud. Dad and his little fire-fighter jokes. Good one, Dad!

Spanky, I've been so angry since I first got here. With the Afghan people. Like it was their fault we were in this war. Like it was their fault I had to be over here, away from you and Mom.

But the other day, we were walking through a village. An Afghan family was huddled in this make-shift tent. I found out later they'd lost their home in a bombing raid by the Taliban.

A boy stuck his head out of the tent to watch us. He spoke English and his name is Rasheed. He's your age, Spanky. Rasheed told me his name meant "powerful."

When he smiled at me, all I could see was you.

What a joke. Rasheed reminds you of me? Yeah. Right. Mr. Powerful loses his home and can still smile? I can't even handle a little razzing at school.

When I looked at Rasheed, when I talked to him, all I could think about was how much I missed you. How much I wanted to be home. And I realized that this war wasn't his fault or his parent's fault.

Make no mistake about it though, Spanky. War is horrible. Don't let anyone tell you differently. People like to think about the heroes and the enemies. But hardly anyone thinks about the innocent people who die in wars.

How's the new school? Do you like your teacher? You must have dozens of friends by now. If not, it'll happen.

How about just one friend, Dad? Huh? How about that? Have I made you proud yet?

I can't decide how Mom sounds on the phone. She tells me you're helping her every day. That's what I'm talking about. Keep it up, son. I knew I could count on you.

Write me when you can. Your letters will make my day. I'll try to send you a photo of my team with our humvee.

I love you.
Dad

I hit the reply button and start typing, without even thinking about what I want to say.

Dear Dad:
Man, I miss you! It's been tough not talking to you or getting email.

Should I tell him about Mom? About her not working sometimes. Or the fire?

Mom made this amazing spaghetti dinner to celebrate you getting back to base. But I knew you'd be back. You can handle things over there. I bet everyone counts on you big time. How many lives have you saved so far?
Not much going on here. Oh, except that something happened to my teacher Miss Anders today. She couldn't breathe and fell on the floor and almost died. But I think she'll be okay. Dar gave her CPR. He's my new friend. There's this kid Mack who makes life kind of tough. But not as tough as what you must be going through.
We have to do reports for Outdoor Ed. I'm doing mine on snakes. Surprise! Okay, I know you could have guessed it.
Mom and I are fine. Seriously. Don't worry about a thing. I'm taking care of everything. We miss you. Write me again soon!
Your son, Spanky.
P.S. I'm trying hard to make you proud.

I almost hit send, but change my mind. I erase the P.S., then add a new one.

P.S. Some kids were talking about the war in the lunchroom. One kid said what you said. That you guys are making us safer by fighting the terrorists. But another kid said his dad thought we had no business being over there.

I just wish you were home. Sorry that it's horrible.

P.S.S. Tell Rasheed a.k.a. "Mr. Powerful" that YOUR SON said, hi.

I wish I had a button that could turn off my brain. Everything that happened today keeps spinning around in my head. Why did I freeze, trying to help Miss A? And my report. Will it be good enough? Mom's happier. For tonight that is. But what will she be like tomorrow? I toss and turn and think about Mack and Miss A and Jazz and then Mack again. I think about Dad hanging with Mr. Powerful. Will he still want me for his son? I end up pulling my sheets into a huge ball.

The volume of the TV in the living room isn't helping. "Tonight, we'll be examining overcrowded classrooms and the growth of private schools—"

Boring. But at least Mom is watching something besides cable news.

"—but first, we'll examine bullies in our public schools. Tonight we'll talk to an expert on the subject in a segment we call, 'The Shadow in Your Child's Classroom.'"

I jump out of bed and slip down the hall.

"We'll be interviewing a leading expert on the subject, Dr. Craig Jandr from the Institute of Behavioral Studies, right after this short network break."

"Hi sweetie," Mom says. "I thought you were asleep."

"Just thirsty."

It takes slow sips of two full glasses of water to hear the interview. I think what Dr. Jandr is trying to say is that there are a lot of reasons a kid becomes a bully. Some of what he says goes right over my head about "family dynamics" and "repressed anger," stuff Dar would understand. Then he says something in plain words, about how some bullies feel small inside. If I understand him right, there can be things going on in the bully's life which are out of his control. (I guess girls can be bullies, too.) Anyway, he says some bullies try to feel bigger by picking on someone they think they can control.

It seems kind of lame. Maybe I'm not understanding it at all. But, Mack Malone feel small? No way. The second half of the interview won't be on for two weeks—the part about what to do if a bully is giving you a hard time. Terrific. Would've been nice to know this before the campout.

Back in bed, I straighten out my sheets, wondering if someday the Doc might talk about why a kid freezes even when he knows what to do. Or how to turn a wuss like me into someone everyone looks up to, like my dad.

144

I guess I fell asleep, cause I just woke up covered with cold sweat and I can't get this dream out of my head.

I'm kneeling by Miss Anders side. She turns into a tiny version of Mack. Then he gets huge and I shrink.

It got really weird after that.

Mack turns back into Miss A, and yells, "Help me, Spanky. I need you to teach Outdoor Ed."

Then Dad walks up, ruffles my hair and says, "Make me proud."

I tell him, "I can't. I have to pee."

Funny thing. I really do have to pee.

Chapter 26
"Fire one!"

I can't believe it when I get to school the next
morning. It's the normal class-without-a-teacher-
waiting-for-the-bell-and-substitute-teacher circus: kids
sitting on top of their desks, eating snacks, throwing
paper planes, doodling on the chalkboard, listening to
music, playing triangle football, texting on cell phones.
And Jazz's seat is empty.

Mack slithers in and checks out everyone. Then he
backs up to the door, peeks up and down the hall.
"Coast's clear," he yells, and climbs on Miss A's chair,
then up on top of her desk. "Looks like we're on our
own, today, boys and girls."

Ned whistles and a bunch of kids start clapping
and pounding on top of their desks. Did I say circus?
Nah. It's more like a zoo. This would never happen
where I used to live.

Mack looks over at Dar and says, "Tough luck, Brain Sludge. Looks like Miss Anders ain't in a big hurry to come back to see you."

Up until that moment, with Jazz out and no sleep, I've been kind of zoning out, watching the show, with my elbows propped on my desk, and my head resting in my hands. But I concentrate hard, sending Dar thought waves. Tell him she's not in any hurry to come back and see you either, puke breath. But Dar just opens a book and ignores him.

"Well, if it isn't the freezer boy," Mack says, turning his attention to me. He jumps off Miss A's desk with a thud from his boots and heads my way. "I was actually beginning to think you had some real grits, Cub Scout." He sits on top of his own desk, his feet on the seat. "You had your chance to make out with Miss Anders, save her life and *evathin*. But noooo. You go and freeze on her!"

Ned howls, but then his expression changes. "You know, Mack. Miss A weally looked bad. I wondaw if she'll kick the bucket."

I don't get Ned. His speech impediment cracks everyone up. But he acts like he doesn't notice. Dar said he heard that since first grade, three speech therapists have given up on him 'cause he kept skipping his appointments.

But Ned's comment about Miss A kicking the bucket shuts everyone up. Everyone except Maggie. "Don't say that, Ned." She pulls her hair back into a ponytail. "You shouldn't be talking about Miss Anders like that."

"And who made you the boss of me?"

Maggie snaps the little stretchy thingy in place, ignoring Ned. She taps Mack's knee and whispers too loudly, "Remember what Dad said. Leave Spanky and Dar alone."

Mack's grin fades fast. "Mind your own business, banana nose."

Maggie's head jerks. "Cut it out, Mack."

"I don't care what Dad says. He can stick it as far as I'm concerned. One of these days he'll get it that I'm me, is all, and he better get used to it. So keep your long nose to yourself."

I pretend to look outside. Jazz still hasn't gotten to school.

I turn back and Maggie's staring at me. "She's at the eye doctor."

How did she know I was looking for Jazz?

The second bell rings and she spins back toward the classroom door. Mack and Ned are firing spitballs at each other, pretending they're soldiers.

It makes me wonder if telling Mack about my dad being overseas would make him leave me alone. Maybe even want to be friends. But it doesn't seem right to use my dad to handle my problems.

Mack yells, "Fire one," and flicks a spitball. Ned ducks and the spitball keeps going, over Ned's head, past two other students, past the last desk near the door, and—

"Good morrrrning, my children."

In walks guess who! Sheesh. Ms. Badu swats her face like there's a gnat bothering her. "Remember me? My name is Ms. Badu. That's baaah like a sheep and do like how doooo you do!"

Chapter 27
Living on the Other Side

Mr. Taylor peeks his head in. He and Ms. Badu hang out at the door, talking quietly, but not quiet enough to keep me from hearing Mr. Taylor say, "...Outdoor Ed. reports are due..."

It's bad enough that we get the sub who yelled at Dar and was nice to Mack. But I'd been hoping for one extra night to go over my report again.

Ms. Badu writes her name on the board again. Then she turns to us and says, "I'll be your sub until Miss Anders returns. That gives us plenty of time to get to know each other. Yes, we'll get to know each other reeeally well."

Sure enough, she announces we'll be giving our reports this morning. Dar raises his hand and Ms. Badu lets him go first. He rolls a projector to the front of the class, and when he connects it to his laptop, his title pops up. "The Effect of Toxic Algae on Florida's Ecosystem. By Dar Garfunkle."

Dar's my friend, but seriously, the beginning of his report almost put me to sleep. Too many charts and graphs. The guy's a human straw who sucks up facts and numbers and spits them back out. I've just never been friends with a guy like him.

But after a little bit, he starts telling a story about how toxic algae are hurting ocean life, and smelling up the beaches from the dead fish and turtles. Makes me sad, thinking of fish and baby turtles washing up on shore to die and smell.

The whole time, Ms. Badu's been watching Mack, who's sitting in his desk like a little angel. Dar finishes, the class claps, and Ms. Badu calls another person who does her report, and another and another. Just before lunch, she looks at me. "Mr. McDougal! I just found Miss Anders' schedule and you were supposed to go first. So why don't you come up here and go next."

I walk up the aisle with my head down, sure my report is going to bomb. I seriously tried to make it interesting and maybe even a little funny, but—

Get a grip. It's good enough. It'll be fine.

I get to the front, stare at my paper, take a deep breath and—

Jazz walks in.

Perfect. I wait for her to sit down and take another deep breath. "'Living on the Other Side' by Spanky McDougal.'"

"SPEAK UP, SON!"

I whirl around. My report flies out of my hand and falls onto Miss A's desk. Ms. Badu hands it back to me, and winks. Then she leans back in her chair, crosses her arms, and closes her eyes.

Now my hands are shaking and I try not to let the paper shake too much but the kids can tell. "When I moved to Appalacheeville," I say louder, "I wondered how this town got its name. Now I know. The Apalachee were a Native American tribe. Apalachee means 'people on the other side.'"

I let it sink in, still looking at my paper so I don't lose my place.

"So, I guess you could say we're a bunch of DIPS living on the other side."

The class giggles.

Crummy joke. But it worked. Yeah, it's going to be okay. The butterflies in my stomach stop flapping their wings and I look up to share the laugh. Instead of seeing smiling faces, everyone's staring at Mack and Ned. Mack has his finger down his throat like he's fake puking. Ned's finger's up his nose, and both of them are making funny faces.

I spin around to look at Ms. Badu who opens her eyes, then winks again. "Please, continue, Mr. McDougal."

So I read. "Living on the other side has its challenges. My report is about one of them.

When you live on the other side here in Appalacheeville, it's a good idea to know your neighbors. I don't mean the little old lady who lives next door. I'm talking reptiles and amphibians. And specifically, snakes."

Again, I hear giggles. I look up hopeful, but again, Mack is stealing my show. He's leaning back in his seat, rocking back and forth with his eyes closed like Ms. Badu and poking Ned with a ruler. I spin around. Ms. Badu's eyes are still shut. She hasn't seen a thing.

I decide right then and there that when I get my first pet snake, I'm going to train him to bite on demand.

I keep reading. "Did you ever wonder how many different kinds of snakes there are in Florida? The answer is 45. But don't let that scare you. Only six are killers: Three are rattlesnakes and they have a rattle on one end to warn us that they're nearby. Here's a Canebrake Rattlesnake."

I hold up a sketch I've drawn. "Canebrakes eat small mammals like rabbits and rats. They also eat birds.

"This drawing is an Eastern Diamondback. Get this: these guys are really shy and like to hide. They only bite if they have to. They'd rather you just go away.

And this one's a Dusky Pygmy Rattlesnake. He's gray with black splotches. Get a good look at him. More people get bit by Pygmies in Florida than any other snake."

Mack is half out of his chair, stretching. He yawns one of those exaggerated kind of yawns the whole class can hear.

It's funny how a yawn like that can make everyone yawn.

I feel sweat drip down my back. But what can I do? I just keep showing my sketches. "The other

153

poisonous snakes in Florida are a Cottonmouth, a Copperhead, and a Coral snake."

Brrrrrrrring.

The lunch bell rings just as I'm about to finish. Ms. Badu finally wakes up to say "That was an interesting report, Spanky."

Everyone's too busy packing and leaving. No one claps. They push by me as if I'm not even there. Mack gets too close and whispers, "Thanks for the nap, Shame us."

Maggie stops. "Um. . . so. . ."

"Huh?" I can't figure out what she's trying to say.

"So. . . so, see ya," she says, and then takes off. Jazz follows her, and never looks back.

Was the report that bad? Oh man, it's just a stupid speech. So why do I feel so lousy?

Before going to lunch, I take my sketches to Art class so I don't have to carry them around all afternoon. Mr. Riley passes me on my way in. "What do you have for me?" he says.

"Is it okay if I set these in here for the afternoon? I know I don't have Art today, but—"

Mr. Riley takes one. "Incredibly accurate, Spanky. A beautiful rendering." He goes through the other sketches and says, "Ok with you if we hang them?"

Mr. Riley is pretty cool. He's the only other person besides my mom who's ever said something nice about my sketches. Thing is, I could draw a stick figure and Mom would like it. Or at least she used to.

Mr. Riley says I have to sign them first. But what should I write? Spanky McDougal? SMcD? SM? I end up signing them "Spanky". Kinda weird. I feel a little taller with each sketch I sign.

It hits me that a certain someone might pay more attention to my work since my snakes will be hanging in her Art class. Yeah, after Mr. Riley, and Art, and hanging up my sketches, giving a stupid report that nobody liked doesn't matter so much now.

Then again, it's not much of a story to tell my dad. Hey Dad, guess what? My Art teacher likes my sketches. Hoo haw.

Chapter 28
Overgrown Bullies

In Afghanistan, there's this place where the wind is a big problem. When it blows, it sprays everything with sand and huge insects. It covers the soldiers. Their food. Inside their beds and clothes. Everything gets covered with sand.

Mom and I are watching a show about it. I think we're both hoping we'll see Dad. No luck. Afterwards, they scroll the names of soldiers who've been killed in combat. The song that goes "Glory, Glory Hallelujah, his truth is marching on," is playing in the background.

I read each name as it slides down the screen. But my mind wanders to imagining Dad carrying soldiers to safety. There's no way any of these people could be on his team. He'd have saved them.

Mom hits the off button on the remote. "I can't bear to watch any more of this."

"Dad's name will never be on that list." I hold one of the little couch pillows to my stomach. "If anyone can take care of those terrorists over there, it's Dad."

"I'm sure you're right, Spanky." She leans over and pats me on the head but I push her hand away. "Did you hear the words in that verse?" I ask, bolting up off the couch. I throw the pillow on the floor. I want to throw the remote through the television screen. "It said something about a hero crushing a serpent with his heel."

Mom just sits there, rubbing her hands like her knuckles hurt or something. I have to get away from her. On my way out of the room, I yell, "They're talking about Dad!"

I turn on my computer to do some history homework and I've got mail. From him.

Dear Spanky:

Hi son! It sounds like you're dealing with some tough stuff. I guess I forgot how hard it can be, starting out in a new school. I want to know more about your classmates.

I thought about what you'd overheard at lunch, about this war. In time, you'll form your own opinions. I guess you hear reports on the news so maybe you already have an opinion. But I want you to know mine.

Before I came here, well, you know I had a lot to say about war. Now, there's little time to think about it. Mostly I think about coming home. I try to believe we're doing the right thing over here for the right reason. Some of the radical groups here act like the worst kind of thugs, Spanky. Thugs are nothing more than overgrown bullies who do terrible things to people.

But after being here a while, it's hard not to wonder if sometimes we're doing the wrong things for the right reason. Sometimes innocent people are hurt. Like Rasheed's family losing their home. But here's the thing, pal. Can we do nothing? Do we help them half-way and come home? Still, how many of our own soldiers do we let die helping other countries? Shouldn't they be helping themselves? Can they help themselves??

All this rambling probably sounds confusing. It is for me too. Especially when you add the problem of protecting our country from terrorists. We'll have to talk about this some more.

I hope Miss Anders recovers quickly. I want to know more about this kid, Mack, too. Some bullies have brains that are messed up. They're bad to the core—the type who grow up to become thugs or serial killers. In that case, you're better off staying clear of him. But other times, a bully may not be as tough as he seems. It can be a big front. Only you can figure out which type of bully this guy Mack is.

When I get back tonight, I'll be looking for your letter with lots of details. I have a lot of writing to make up to you. I promise—as soon as I get your reply, I'll write you right back immediately or as soon as I wake up. Either way, you'll have a reply before you go to school. We'll figure it all out. So check your mail in the morning.

I love you, son.

Dad.

P.S. Mom tells me over and over how much you're helping at home. Thanks, Buddy. You're one heck of a soldier's son.

I hit reply and my fingers start flying, just like my old teacher, Ms. Appelt, used to say when we had to do a book report. "Write like your fingers are on fire!" I tell Dad all about Mack. Like how he's giving my new friend *Dar* a tough time about being a Boy Scout, and how he tripped *Dar* in the hall. And how he never leaves *Dar* alone.

I know he promised to write me back right away, but I can't take any chances. I add a P.S.

Dar really needs to know what to do. Please write back immediately so I can tell him at school tomorrow.

Chapter 29
In Heaven?

When I walk in the kitchen the next morning, Mom is smiling, but looks like she hasn't slept at all. She has those dark circles under her eyes again. There's a box on the table. "I've been working on this care package all night," she says. "Want to add anything?"

I run back to my room and get a pair of jeans I've outgrown. I quickly check my email, but there's no reply from Dad about what Dar should do. On a piece of paper, I write, "These are for Mr. Powerful. Tell him I'm really sorry he lost his house."

At school, Ms. Badu calls the roll and goes over our schedules. Then she suddenly looks at her watch. "Class, I almost forgot. Now don't be getting all pea-brained on me, but I have an announcement. Mr. Blowford has picked your class to attend the DIP Kindergarten Grandparents Day Sing-Along."

You'd think everyone just got food poisoning with all the moans.

"From what I understand, this is an annual tradition. Mr. Blowford invites one middle or upper school class to walk across the parking lot for this Sing-Along. I bet those rug rats will be excited to have you there to watch them. And I expect you to behave like grownups."

Ned raises his hand and asks, "Ms. Badu, do we weally have to go? Can some of us go to the libwawy instead?"

She shakes her head. "Here's what's going to happen. You're going to put your books in your lockers and meet in front of our building at 8:30 am. That's five minutes from now, so no fooling around. Anyone who doesn't show up will have an automatic detention in Mr. Blowford's office."

The tiny furniture in the Kindergarten building reminds me of when I was a little kid. My dad used to come meet me for lunch. He looked so funny sitting in the baby chairs. Trying to fit my butt into one of them reminds me I'm not that little kid anymore.

On the stage, a white-haired lady's playing *I'm a Little Teapot* on this big 'ole grand piano. Suddenly, she changes songs to *You're a Grand Old Flag* and a line of tiny kids march on the stage. Some adults help them climb on the tiers of seats next to the piano.

Mack's making a big show of rolling his eyes and pointing at one little guy holding a miniature flag. Now he's laughing at the kid and waving his own pretend flag! A teacher storms his way.

Piano lady ends up stopping that teacher in her tracks when she says, "Welcome everyone, to the David I. Patrick Kindergarten Sing-Along. Abbie Riley? Will you please come forward, dear?"

A little girl wearing a pink dress walks up to her. She looks around the room and runs back to her seat. One of the adults takes her hand and leads her back to the center of the stage.

Piano-lady says, "Ladies and gentleman, we have a special treat today. Abbie's father, Sergeant Donald Bartow, is a soldier who's been serving in the Middle East. But today, Sergeant Bartow is home on leave and here with us."

She points to a man standing by the cafeteria door. "Abbie tells us her dad isn't wearing his uniform because he can't find one of his boots this morning."

A bunch of people laugh. Abbie giggles. Sergeant Bartow smiles. Then all of the parents and teachers start clapping. A few stand up, and soon, everyone is standing and clapping.

Sergeant Bartow turns to the audience and salutes. It hits me that if I was the same age as Abbie, Miss Anders might be calling me up there. It would be my dad, standing by the door. Imagining him here, wearing his uniform makes my heart slam against my ribs. For some reason, I don't feel so mad at him for leaving anymore. I stick out my chest and clap harder than I've ever clapped before.

Abbie leads us in the pledge of allegiance. Afterwards, Piano lady says, "Please remain standing. Johnny Evans, will you please come stand by me?"

The boy with the tiny flag, the one Mack was laughing at walks up to her. He can't be taller than my waist. He has brown hair that curls all over his head. Kind of looks like a little kid's doll.

"Johnny's father, Private James Evans, also served his country overseas for six months." Piano lady starts playing the music to, "*God Bless America*," and I think, yep, if it was a different time, I could be holding a little flag and Piano lady could be talking about my dad.

But then Piano lady says, "Today, Private Evans is in heaven," and without even taking a breath, she starts singing, "God bless America, land that I..."

Some people sing with her. But a lot of other people are looking around, to their left and right. Their faces look all wrinkled or maybe a little pale. Their eyes are getting all teary, and they act like they don't know what to do. Little Johnny stands on the stage, staring into the crowd. Soon, almost everyone is singing while Little Johnny waves his flag back and forth.

I hear voices around me, but it's as if I'm underwater or my ears are full of cotton. Heaven? Johnny's dad is in heaven?

At the water fountain outside the kiddie lunchroom, I crouch down to get a drink. With each gulp, I get madder. It's not another year. I'm not in kindergarten. And it's not my dad. My dad's a firefighter.

He saves lives. He knows how to take care of himself. Nothing's going to happen to him.

Walking back to our building, the air seems sticky, like I'm in a bubble of syrup. A crowd of kids move me forward. Someone slams the bar to open the door and the cold air-conditioned air wakes me up.

Yeah. My dad knows how to take care of himself.

Back in my seat, I remember that I never got an email from him this morning. I feel a little sleepy and rest my eyes. I see Abbie's Dad saluting and little Johnny waving his flag. Probably just couldn't get a turn on the computer. I rest my head on my arms. The heat must be making me—

"Wake up, Spanky."

"Huh?" I shake my head.

Maggie's tapping me on the shoulder. "Sorry. But I think you were talking in your sleep."

It takes a second for my eyes to focus. Ms. Badu is taking the purple marker from Mack. "Good work, Professor Malone," she says. "Just a hunch. But you're a lot smarter than you want to let on. From now on, let's see you use a little more of that brain of yours. It might keep you from digging yourself into a hole— you know what happens when you dig yourself into a hole full of trouble, don't you?"

Mack's face looks clueless.

"You might not be able to climb your way out of it, son."

Mack's mouth curls as he heads back to his seat. Along the way, he mutters, "Yeah, riiiight. As if there's a hole this soldier can't climb out of."

"And good morning, Spanky!"

I look up real quick. Ms. Badu is staring at me.

"Glad to see you're back with us, son,"

Strange. She's smiling. She doesn't look mad.

"Oh and Spanky, stop by my desk sometime when you have a few extra minutes. We need to have a little talk."

Brrrrriiiiiig! Brrrrriiiiiig! Brrrrriiiiiig!

"Well. Lucky day. Let's hope this is just a drill," says Ms. Badu, grabbing her rainbow purse. "Students! Line up quickly."

Brrrrriiiiiig! Brrrrriiiiiig! Brrrrriiiiiig!

"We're going to march outside in single file and I expect you to hold your tongues the whole way."

As soon as we push through the doors to the field, the hot humid air nearly knocks me over. The sun is high overhead and everything looks too white and glary. By the time we reach the basketball courts, my tee-shirt's all sweaty. Blowfish is at one end of the courts in his brown suit, yelling through a megaphone about fire safety. I yank on Dar's sleeve and motion for him to follow me to the oak tree. We'll still look like we're in line with our class, just a little farther away.

165

"What do you think Ms. Badu wants to talk to me about?"

Dar's eyes dart back and forth between our class and me. "How about sleeping in class?"

"I was hot. And tired. I started thinking about—" My mind went blank again. What had I been thinking about before I nodded off?

"You started thinking about what?" Dar throws his hands up in the air. "Seriously, Spanky. I'm starting to worry about you. Maybe you should talk to my dad."

"Your dad? Why would I want to talk to him?"

Dar shrugs. "He's a psychologist. You know, a shrink."

"I know what a shrink is," I say, remembering that my mom used to see one. Maybe I'm just a chip off the 'ole block. Maybe I'll end up sleeping all the time like her. That'll make Dad real proud.

I can't look at Dar. "Way to make me feel worse," I say. "You think I'm going nuts?"

"I'm sorry," he says, and pushes my shoulder. "Look. Ms. Badu doesn't seem to appreciate me and we could get in trouble standing here. I'm heading back."

I wave him off and kneel at the bottom of my shady tree. Maybe Dar is right. I've been freezing up every time I need to do something. I'm falling asleep in class. And now my mind is going blank on me. Maybe I am going a little crazy.

Chapter 30
You Are Under the Spell

I lean back against the big 'ole oak tree. The class is in a long straggly line, ending not too far from me. Jazz is talking to Dar. Again. Sheesh.

I close my eyes and imagine her waving goodbye to Dar and walking up to me. She asks if she can sit next to me. I say—

Glory, Glory, Hallelujah...his truth is marching on.

It's that song again. But where is it? It sounds like it's coming from someone's house near the school. I pull myself up and hang from a low branch. The muscles in my arms sure look puny. Compared to Mack's ropey arms, mine look like twine. Maybe more pull ups. That's one. Two. Okay, almost two.

Blowford's still barking through his megaphone. So I plop back down, lean against the trunk and try to go back to my Jazz dream. Crunching footsteps interrupt me again. It's Mack and Ned. But they haven't noticed me sitting around the other side.

"...I'll tell you, Ned, but ah jeez, you're never going to believe it."

If Mack finds me, he'll think I'm purposefully spying on him. I start whistling that Glory Hallelujah song to make sure he knows someone's here.

Mack snaps, "Who's that?" They both come around to my side of the tree. "Oh, it's just McLoser."

Ned starts hopping from one foot to the other like he has ants in his pants. "Come on, Mack. Tell me!"

"Swear on my mother's grave you'll never tell anyone what I'm gonna tell you."

Mack is always swearing on his mom's grave. I wonder if she hears him. He looks at me again, rolls his eyes and gets that tough look on his face.

"That goes for you, too, Butt-face."

Ned crosses his heart with his finger and says, "Come on alweady. Spill it!"

Mack turns to Ned so his back is to me. "So Ms. Badu calls me up."

"Yeah, I remembaw," Ned says. "So what?"

I can't hear what Mack says next, so I try another pull up. "Two."

Mack looks at me and his voice gets louder. "She keeps nodding at me. Nodding and smiling. It's like she's inside my head again; I tell you there's something strange about that teacher. I couldn't believe it. I start remembering stuff we learned."

"Three." I can't hear the rest of what he tells Ned.

168

All of a sudden Mack grabs him around the thighs and lifts him in the air. "She makes me feel smart. With that kind of smarts, I bet the Army'll want me, big time."

I let go of the branch and land. Ned's fists are flying, beating Mack on the back. "Put me down, you fweak."

"And like I always tell ya, Ned—" Mack says, setting Ned back down.

"When you join the Awmy, no mawe Dad."

"That's my ticket," Mack says, and high fives Ned.

After seeing how Mack's dad had treated him in the car, I can understand why he wants to get away from him. But then, it's not like Mack doesn't deserve what his dad gave him.

Brrrrriiiiig! Brrrrriiiiig! Brrrrriiiiig!

Mack looks over his shoulder. "Hey McFrugal. I catch you mouthing anything I said, I'll flatten your sorry butt, hear me?"

"Mouthing what? I didn't hear anything," I say, but cross my fingers behind my back.

Mack watches me when I catch up with Dar. So I wait to say anything. After school, I call him, but he's at the library. I email him. Still no letter back from Dad.

Mom's fixing tomato soup and grilled cheese sandwiches. That's a good sign. At least she's making dinner and not sleeping. Maybe she's on her way up the rollercoaster ride she always seems to be on.

Then again, she usually fixes grilled cheese and tomato soup when she's trying to make me feel better. Like when I cut my hair by myself and learned I didn't know how.

Her eyes look like Dad's did the day he left—the little lines under her bottom lids make her look so tired. I know I should be thankful she had one up day, but what if her seesaw stays stuck in the down position? It's freaky having her being sad so much all by myself.

I scoop a spoonful of soup and hold it up. "I wonder how they make tomato soup," I say, to get her mind off things. "Do you think they throw a ton of tomatoes in a big vat and people mush them around with their feet? You know, like the way Dad said people used to make wine."

"Maybe," but she just stares into her bowl.

"Yeah, I guess that's pretty gross." I try again. "Our new sub, Ms. Badu is kind of weird, Mom."

"How so?"

"She's...different." I tell her all about "big 'ole Badu,' even that she wants to talk to me sometime. I figure it'll make her curious enough to pull it out of me.

But Mom's eyes are glazed. "That's nice, Spanky. Be sure to talk to her."

Mom hasn't eaten anything. She just keeps stirring her soup with her spoon. "It's. . . it's. . . everything's going to be okay."

"Exactly. Dad's just out on patrol."

Whatever I said was totally wrong. Mom starts sobbing. Her whole body is shaking. I move my chair closer to her. Scratch my hand. I catch myself pushing my fingers through my hair, like Dad used to do when he was upset. "Mom?"

"What if Dad is missing, Spanky?"

Here she goes again. I know I'm supposed to let her talk. I know Dad said to be patient with her. But it's driving me crazy.

"Mom, we knew there'd be times when we wouldn't hear from him. Remember what he said. He told us that. That he'd be on patrol. Or maybe he didn't get a turn to use the computer. Why can't you imagine that instead?" I shove my chair away and pick up my bowl.

Later, Dar calls me back. When I finish telling him about Mack's story, about how Ms. Badu has gotten inside his head and made him smart all of a sudden, Dar starts making these sounds. "Bwwaaah...Hooo hooo hah hah heee heee...Mack Malone, you are under the spell of Ms. Badu."

I burst out laughing, thinking Dar could actually be funny. But he keeps at it. "Ms. Badu has put a hex on you, too, Spanky. Dum-di-dum-dum. No, wait. I know. It must be the purple marker. Weird things happen to those who touch it!"

It hits me that Dar isn't just making fun of Ms. Badu or Mack. He's making fun of me. "Some friend you are. I knew you'd think this was nuts."

"Sorry, Spank." The phone goes dead for a minute, except for the sound of Dar's breathing. "Seriously, Spank. You really need to chill out. Get some sleep and forget about all of this."

"But—"

"Or like I said. Maybe talk to someone. See a counselor, Spanky. Seriously."

"Yeah, maybe you're right."

"By the way, I don't know if it's okay to ask, but what have you heard from your dad?"

"We emailed for a couple days, but he was supposed to write me back last night and he didn't," I say, staring at my email folder. "And my mom—" In a flash, I decide not to tell Dar about how bad she gets. How she's going back in that dark place she goes. Then I'll have to listen to him tell me that she needs to see a shrink too. But I have to finish the sentence so I say something that doesn't sound like a big deal. "For some reason, my mom keeps zoning out when I talk to her."

"Like Mother, like Son," Dar says.

"Cut it out, okay?" I want to hang up on him, but his voice tells me he's doing what Dad calls busting my chops. That he's kidding me because he cares about me. "Listen, I gotta go. See you tomorrow."

All I want to do is go to bed. But sometime during the night, Ms. Badu got in my head and made it hard to sleep.

Chapter 31
Glory, Glory Hallelujah

I wait in the boys' bathroom. When Dar turns the corner, I pull him inside, searching stall to stall to make sure the coast is clear. "Dar, you are NOT going to believe the dream I had last night."

"Okay, okay...take a breath, Spank."

I can't get the words out fast enough. "Ms. Badu is standing next to you in the hallway. She's humming a song. I think it was *Glory, Glory Hallelujah*. Yeah, that's what it was.

"Glory Hallelujah? You mean the *Battle Hymn of the Republic?*"

"It's not important, Dar. So Mack comes up, razzes you about how he's smarter than you—"

"Oh really?" Dar's eyes turn to slits. "And what precisely did he say?"

"I don't really remember. That's not important either. Just listen! At first...well, you know...you're a little upset. Ok, you're a lot upset. But then Ms. Badu gives you one of her huge smiles and winks at you. She keeps nodding at you to look at Mack. All of a sudden, Mack shrinks into a little kid, sucking his thumb and blubbering like he wants his mommy or something. And then, you kneel down and pat his head."

"Hmmm." Dar stares at the floor, rubbing his chin. "You say Mack appeared to be a small child?"

"Yeah. What do you think it means?"

"Wanting his mommy. And I'm patting his head. Interesting. Your dream actually makes a great deal of sense. I like it! In fact, it gives me an idea!"

The first bell jolts us. "We'll talk later," he says, and we whip around the entrance to the bathroom and run down the hall to class.

Mack's standing in his usual place outside the door. He has that look in his eyes and sticks out his arm, blocking the doorway. "Hey there, Petboy," he says to Dar, not letting him by. "Now that Miss Anders is out, I bet you're gonna kiss up to Ms. Badoodoo. Ain't that right, Petboy?"

Dar's gaze meets Mack's, but Dar doesn't look irritated or scared. He's looking at Mack like he's looking at a kid in kindergarten. Dar kind of rocks on his heels and smiles. He stands a little taller. Tilts his head to the side. Shocker of all shockers, he says, "Excellent idea, Mackie. She is kinda cool. I think I'll do that," and quickly slips under Mack's arm. Mack looks, well, surprised. Before he can react, I slip through right behind Dar.

The bell rings, and Ms. Badu sings, "Good mooorning, my children," in that deep, happy voice. She walks up to the front of my row and gives me one of her huge smiles. "And how are you today, Spanky?" She looks at me for too long, and finally says, "Did you sleep well last night?"

Then she starts humming *Glory, Glory, Hallelujah.*

Dar's head spins around toward mine. He looks as shocked as I feel. Maybe I'm going crazy. But maybe Ms. Badu has been mixing things up too. Ms. Badu and her purple marker and making Mack smart. Maybe she is some kind of a witch who can get into kid's heads!

I expect to see something in Dar's face that tells me he's thinking the same thing. But his shocked look falls away. Now he's grinning and shaking his head from side to side as if he knows exactly how it happened. Then he mouths, "Bwwaaa...Hooo hooo hah hah heee heee. . ."

Sometime before lunch, Ms. Badu tells us we can work on tonight's homework—we're supposed to research Apalachuway Park and make a list of possible animals and plants we'll see there. I reach under my seat for my notebook and when I sit back up, she's standing at my desk, which pretty much takes up the whole aisle as big as she is. "Mr. Spanky, could you step outside with me for a second?"

Out in the hall, I lean up against a row of lockers. "Did I do something?"

"No, son. I just thought I'd check in with you. When we came back from the sing along, you looked like

175

you sang away a quart of blood, you were so pale. You want to tell me about it?"

The look on her face tells me she won't believe it if I just say I'm fine. Figuring Dar must know what he's talking about, I say, "I think I need to see a shrink."

"A shrink. Hmmm. You mean like a counselor. Aha." Ms. Badu's head keeps nodding. She looks down at her feet and asks, "Everything okay at home? Your mom and dad are okay?"

"No. I mean, yes." And for some reason, I start upchucking words. "Well, I don't like to talk about it but my dad's in Afghanistan. He's a fireman. Then his unit got called up. But he's used to saving people. And Mom's a mess. Kind of worried all the time. He doesn't call or write and she thinks he's missing."

"You do have a few things on your mind," she says, still nodding. "And what about you. Are you worried?"

The lights must have gone out in the hallway. It feels smaller. My breathing isn't working so well and my underarms are getting all sweaty. I just want to go back to my seat, or better yet, to an early lunch.

She tilts her head. "You'll talk about it when you're ready."

"There's nothing to talk about. My dad's not going to end up on a list on TV or like that little kid with the flag's dad. See my dad is counting on me and if I start worrying about him, well, then maybe he will, I mean maybe end up on some list."

176

Miss Badu's eyes kind of grab hold of my eyes and won't let go. "Let me get this straight. You think if you worry about your dad that means he might need to be saved. And if he needs to be saved, he won't be able to save someone else?"

"That's right," I say, relieved. Ms. Badu gets it. I'm thinking there could be something to this witch thing. And if she is a witch, she's a good one. She might not be such a bad sub after all.

"You head on to lunch, Spanky. But we're not done talking."

Terrific.

Chapter 32
Vice President Al Gore?

The next day, Ms. Huntley sends me a note inviting me to come by for a "chat." Still no email from Dad. But I really don't want to "chat" about that. The camping trip is less than a week away. I still don't know what to think about Ms. Badu. I know she's really not a witch. But she's sure changed Mack. He acts different around her. Dar doesn't know how to act around her. Just being smart doesn't impress her much.

Before lunch today, Dar stops me. "Spanky. Help me move this to my Gifted class." He really outdid himself on this project. Used wood to frame three posters and hinged the frames together. Each side closes to the center. The title on the center frame says, "INCONVENIENT?" and it's all about global warming. We each grab an end and head down the long hallway to his class.

No one at DIP knows about geology or the environment better than Dar. And everyone's heard his

Al Gore story. Supposedly, Dar wrote to Vice President Gore, (well he used to be Vice-President a long time ago) to ask him questions about some movie he'd made called "An Inconvenient Truth." But Vice-President Gore never wrote him back. Supposedly, he called him instead. On the phone!

Dar says they talked for an hour about how the earth's temperature was increasing every year. And how the ice caps were melting and the oceans were rising. And supposedly, Mr. Al Gore told Dar it was possible that Appalacheeville could become beachfront property if that happened. He said the world needed more kids like Dar—kids who cared. Dar said he promised the Vice President he'd work on global warming.

Yeah, Dar's a maniac on the subject. And if you ask me, he'll probably come up with something to fix it.

The framing makes this project seriously heavy. "Hold up a second," I say, shaking out my hand. "So, do you want to come over tonight? We can make a list of gear to take on the camping trip."

"Definitely. I'll get my mom to drive me over right after dinner."

The thought of getting ready for the trip puts me in a great mood. Yeah, I might even be feeling a little spunky. And when I see Maggie and Jazz in the lunchroom later, I walk right up and look for a seat close by.

"Hey Spanky!"

Both of them said hi! As soon as I sit down, they go back to talking to each other.

I pretend like I'm not paying attention to them and take out my peanut butter and jelly sandwich, open my milk carton and my book, when Maggie says, "So . . .Um. . .I've been. . ."

She's sitting across the table from me to the left. Jazz is sitting right next to me. Her elbow could touch my elbow. I turn to look at her, but she's nodding at Maggie. She mouths, "Go on."

Maggie asks, "So . . . so what are ya reading, Spanky?"

"Jasper Dash's Flame Pit of Delaware."

"No way. I love M.T. Anderson. He's sooo funny."

Terrific. Maggie loves my favorite author. So I turn back to Jazz and ask, "Who's your favorite author?"

Jazz has this kind of "huh?" expression on her face. She says, "I'm not much of a reader, but—"

"So Spanky." Maggie doesn't let her finish. "Have you noticed anything unusual about Ms. Badu?"

Notice anything unusual? Like everything, maybe. But I'm not quite ready to admit it, at least not yet. "Like what?"

"I don't know. Ms. Badu's. . .different. She kind of shakes everything up." Maggie leans across the table. She's looking straight at me. "Know what I mean, Spanky?"

Maggie's eyes have specs inside the green part. Now she's smiling. I can't stop myself from smiling back. "Yeah, I guess I do."

"Me, too, Spanky," says Jazz.

I take a quick sip of milk so I won't choke. I love it when Jazz says my name.

"Like the first time she was here," Jazz says. "She sure put Mack in his place and didn't let him get the best of her."

I had a mouth full of sandwich, so I just shake my head, yes.

"Then she made Mack the teacher and all of a sudden, Mack acts like he might actually have a brain in his head."

I'm still nodding.

"And yesterday, she suggested we sit with you. You must have gone outside or something."

Peanut butter sticks to the roof of my mouth. So that's why she's talking to me. Ms. Badu asked her to. Terrific.

"But today, surprise, surprise, here you are and you end up liking the same books as Maggie."

Maggie suddenly blurts out, "My mom used to talk about stuff like that. She called it serendipity."

I manage to swallow. "Saran who?"

"Ser-en-dip-ity. It's like when you're doing one thing and something else wonderful happens that you didn't expect."

"Exactly," says Jazz. "Ms. Badu encourages us to sit together, and Spanky learns something new and wonderful." Then Jazz puts her hand on my arm.

I can't believe it. Her ring-covered fingers are touching my arm.

"You learn that Maggie likes—the same books you do."

Maggie's cheeks get all red. What's that about? "Yeah, well maybe we can swap books sometime," I say, not knowing what the heck to do. Then I look at my watch. "Well, I gotta go. I'm supposed to meet Dar and I'm late. See you guys."

I jump up from the table and just about run to the garbage can where I dump my half-eaten sandwich which is the stupidest thing I can do cause now I'm going to be hungry all afternoon and when I'm hungry I get all cranky and who knows if Mom will even fix dinner tonight.

I run out of the cafeteria and on the other side of the door, I realize how stupid I must have just looked. If I was supposed to meet Dar five minutes after I sat down, why did I sit in the first place? They're going to know I made that up and think I'm some weird weenie. I trudge down the hall to where Dar is "Eating with Einstein" and wait for the bell.

As soon as he walks out, I start yammering, "So, I'm sitting next to Maggie and Jazz and..." I spill everything.

"Well, it appears the tables are beginning to turn for you, Spanky. Yesterday, you were happy to be a fly on the lunchroom wall. Today, you find the guts to sit with Maggie and Jazz. Not only does Jazz talk to you, you learn that Maggie likes the same books as you."

"Very funny. But what do you think about the Ms. Badu part. About how both Maggie and Jazz think Ms.

Badu is different. Maybe Mack's right. Maybe she really is some kind of witch. Well, not really a witch, but you know; maybe she has special powers."

Dar rubs his chin. "Perhaps she's an alien." His face looks serious. Then he bursts out laughing. "Spanky. Have you called a shrink yet?"

"Stop it, will you? You think you know everything. Explain how Ms. Badu ended up humming that Glory Hallelujah song she'd hummed in my dream?"

"A simple coincidence. It is likely that both of you heard the same song playing on TV. So you dreamed about it and she ended up humming it."

"Maybe." He made sense. Ms. Badu could have seen the same show Mom and I did, or heard the song during the fire drill. "But, what about Mack growing a brain after she let him be the teacher?" As soon as the words slip out of my mouth, I know I'm a weird weenie. "You're probably right. Maybe I am going nuts. Look, I'll see you later. Still coming over?"

"Sure," he says, walking off. "Why wouldn't I?" Dar pushes through a set of double doors. They slam shut and he's gone.

Why wouldn't you? I yell inside my head. You wouldn't because nothing is turning out the way I hoped since I got to this stupid town. Dad shipping out. Miss Anders getting sick. Me freezing up and spacing out every time I need to do something important. Mom always thinking Dad is missing in action. Ms. Badu liking Mack and dissing you, Dar. But not Jazz. No, Dar. Jazz seems to like you just fine. Not to mention, you think I'm nuts. I just want my old life back. Before we moved. Before Dad left.

I head to my locker to pick up a sketch I want to take to Art. As I'm closing the locker door, Ms. Badu pokes her head out of our classroom. I throw open my locker again, to keep her from seeing me and wonder why I just did that.

Soon enough, the smell of cookies and flowers drifts away. I let out a lungful of air, slam the door shut, and walk right into her.

Chapter 33
Garbage on the Brain

"Well, hello Mr. Spanky McDougal."

"Oh! Hi Ms. Badu. I'm kind of in a little bit of a hurry, so—"

"Take a breath, son, and talk to me for a minute. What do you hear from your dad?"

Here we go. "My dad? Um. I haven't heard from him in a few days. But I'm sure he's just doing his job. Probably on an important mission or something."

"Hmmm...I see. How's your mom doing?"

"My mom's . . . I don't know. Maybe she needs to see a shrink, too."

Ms. Badu looks at the floor as if she's thinking deep thoughts. "Must be hard on you."

"Yes, ma'am, I mean, no. No it's not. Not at all. No, really. I don't have it hard. If you want to know what's hard, it's being in Afghanistan. That's hard. Or, or, losing your home to a bomb and living in a tent. That's hard. And anyway, like I said, my dad can take care of everything. He doesn't need me worrying about him."

She looks up, but kind of looks just past me. Then she says, "Well, I bet he's proud of you, too, son."

I scuff the floor with my sneaker. "I'm working on that. Working on that real hard."

When I look back up, her eyes lock on to mine. "Ever think maybe you're working on it a little too hard?"

"Um. I don't know. I don't think so. I'm not really doing too well at it."

"I see." She stares at the floor again, and keeps saying, "Hmm. Hmmm. Hmm." When she finally looks back at me, her mouth is stretched into a big 'ole Ms. Badu smile. "You know what, son? I have a hunch. Do you remember a long time ago, I told you that maybe your insides were affecting your outsides?"

"Yes, ma'am. Didn't really know what you meant though."

"Uh huh. Well let me see how I can explain it. Try to imagine worries like a bag of garbage sitting on top of your brain."

"A garbage bag." I repeat, so she knows I'm listening, even though it sounds crazy.

"Now this garbage bag can only hold so much. But let's say you happen to have a lot of worries. So you shove the garbage down to make room for all of them. If you put too many worries in that bag, well then it starts leaking out the bottom and overflowing out the top."

"Yes, ma'am," I say, beginning to imagine what she's saying.

186

She stops smiling. "The thing is, son, plain and simple. Having your Dad away from home can be tough. Throw that into that garbage bag sitting on your brain and it's enough to fill it pretty full. So you push it down to the bottom of your bag. But your dad's not just far away, he's fighting in a war. It doesn't matter if he's a hero. It's still a scary thing. Add that to your garbage bag."

My chest feels tight. Just like Mack said, she's looking inside my head. How do I get away from her?

"Now in your case, you've got the usual worries that come with being the new kid at school. So throw that in with the other worries. It's not like your bag isn't full enough already. Now it's overfilled, don't you think?"

She's definitely gotten into my head now and she's reading my mind. She can see into every secret thought. But it's like she found a loose thread, hanging from my brain. She's pulling it and I'm starting to unravel.

"I guess," I say.

Ms. Badu's eyes are glued to mine. They feel kind of like a hug, though, but without touching. Her voice is soft. "Your mom's having a tough go of it. And on top of everything else, you're trying to make your dad proud. And you think you're not doing too well at it. I'd say that bag of worries must be leaking and overflowing all over the place by now."

If anything's leaking, it's my eyes, so I try to look away and nod my head, like a bobble head again.

"You've got a lot weighing on that head of yours. Worrying about your dad doesn't mean you think less of him. It doesn't mean that anyone else will either. And no one will think anything less of you if you need to talk about it. Am I making any sense?"

More head bobbles,

"Sometimes, son, you just have to take some of those worries out of the bag. You do that by talking about them. There happens to be a lot of kids with Moms and Dads serving overseas. I bet they'd like to talk to you.

More bobbles.

"I'm here for you, anytime. You understand?"

More bobbles as she walks away. I've been holding my breath the whole time. When she's finally out of sight, I let it out, and I have to take another breath real quick.

I've been under water way too long.

Chapter 34
Dad Worry?

I check my email later. Just a note from Dar saying he can't come over, but nothing from Dad. So I write him.

Dear Dad,

I guess you're still busy doing your job. You probably should know that Mom's pretty worried about you. I'm trying not to be. I bet you're the most PREPARED soldier over there. It's just that I've got a few things leaking out of my brain. So get back to base soon. And write me as soon as you do, okay?

Your number one son, Spanky.

P.S. I sent Mr. Powerful a pair of my old jeans. I hope they fit him.

After mowing the lawn and making boxed macaroni and cheese for Mom and me, I check my mailbox again. Nothing.

But then right before bed, there's an email from Dad! The subject line says, *SAFE AND SOUND*.

Dear NUMBER ONE Son:

I don't know where to begin. First, I'm really sorry I didn't write you back right away the other night, like I said I would. We were supposed to be back in six hours. It's very late, but I finally got my turn to use the computer. You and mom must be pretty worried. I know I would be.

I stopped reading for a second. Dad worry? Since when?

We were out on patrol when a group of Afghani children ran out to us. (Not Rasheed.) Spanky, the kids looked so dirty and skinny. They were begging for food. We gave them some of our rations and candy. All of a sudden, insurgents (that's a group of thugs) surrounded us. All I could think about was you and Mom back home. About how much I wanted to be back there with you. I can tell you son, I've been afraid many times in my life, but nothing compared to how scared I was at that moment.

Dad afraid?
My dad?
But then, who wouldn't be in that situation?

*The main thing I want to tell you, Spanky, is that
we prepared for situations like the one we were in. Once I
focused on that, I was able to put my fear in its place. So I
could do what was needed. There's so much more to tell
you, but I'm fine. I'm back at base, tired, but happy.*

*Now let's talk about you and this brain leaking you
mentioned. I'll be on base for some R&R, so tell me
EVERYTHING that's going on with you.*

Love, Dad

*P.S. I'll tell Rasheed about the jeans when I see him
again.*

I hit REPLY almost immediately.

Dear Dad,

Since he's resting and recuperating, he'll probably
enjoy a nice long letter. So I tell him EVERYTHING. My
brain is moving like . . .like it's rushing over a waterfall
or something. Words are pouring through my fingertips
onto the keyboard. I wipe my eyes with my sleeve.
Between you and me, they're pouring too.

I tell him about the first day I met Dar on the bus
and us being scouting buddies. And that it's been Dar
AND me who Mack is giving a hard time. I tell him about
Miss A's heart attack, only this time I tell him the truth.
That I tried to help her but ended up freezing. I write
about my not-so-funny Outdoor Ed report. And about
Professor Malone, and how I froze trying to write
Preparation on the board.

191

I fill him in on my new almost friends, Maggie and Jazz, about how Maggie likes to read the same books as me but that Jazz is an artist just like me. I even tell him that I'm hoping the Outdoor Ed trip will get Jazz to really notice me. I tell him about Mack's dad and what I saw, and about Dar thinking I need to see a shrink.

Writing about Ms. Badu takes up a lot of space. Explaining to Dad what she told me about worries, well, I think I really get it now.

I hit "Send," dive onto my bed, and somehow, the sky has changed from pitch black to gray and it's already morning. I feel wide awake. I think I've lost a few pounds too. Talking to Dad sure helped me take out the garbage. And just in time for the Outdoor Ed campout.

First thing this morning, Ms. Badu parades us to the auditorium for a camping trip assembly. She says she has to cover a class for another teacher and will be back after it's over. Dar and I sit together. Mack and Ned are two rows in front of us. And man, are we excited about the weekend. It's like someone in the room put their finger in an electrical socket and we're all getting the jolt.

Mack stands and does one of his huge exaggerated yawns, twisting in every direction. He spots Dar and me. "Hey Four Eyes," he says to Dar. "How you gonna find your way in the woods with those binoculars you call glasses? Let me guess, your pal Butt-face McDougal is going to be your seeing eye-dog."

Dar leans forward and smiles. "Good one, Mackie. Actually, I thought I'd bring my night-vision goggles. I think you'd like them."

Eyes pop. Jaws drop everywhere. Dar has fended off another Mack attack. Mack's face turns red and you can tell he's gritting his teeth. Then he says, "Yeah right. Night-vision goggles. No way."

"Yes indeedy. Zisenell NVG9 Vipers—just like the ones they used to use in the Army. They even have a head strap. My uncle gave them to me when he quit hunting."

The word Army must have sunk in. Mack's eyes bulge a little. "I've got a great idea," he says. "Why don't you ditch Buttsky McDougal and bunk with Ned and me?"

Then he looks at me and laughs his guts out.

Chapter 35
What Condition?

Mr. Taylor reminds everyone about our packing lists, trip rules, that boys will bunk with boys, girls with girls, chaperones, and blah blah blah. Dar and I had already decided we were going to wait it out. If he counted right, there would be one tent with just two guys, and we wanted the two to be him and me.

Back in class, it's the last day before the trip and I swear the clock hands need oiling. This morning is lasting forever. The lunch bell finally rings, but Ms. Badu stops me on my way out. "Spanky. Let me have a word with you."

I turn halfway around, but take a few more steps toward the door.

"Pay attention out there on your camp out."

"Yes, ma'am!" I say, and turn the rest of the way around. She's pulled a smile out of me again, so I say, "I threw out the garbage, Ms. Badu. Still need to work on Mom, but I can't wait to be in the woods."

In that voice that works its way through my ears all the way to my toes, she says, "Here's my last bit of advice. Get out there, take in that fresh air, and..."

"And?" I say, wondering what strange thing was coming next.

"And have a good time. Do you hear me, son?"

"YES MA'AM!" I run out the door. Instead of going to lunch, I stop at my locker just as Dar flies around the corner.

"Where were you?" he yells, "I've been looking all over for you."

"Ms. Badu made me stay after class.

"Listen, I'm late for Gifted. Meet me after school. We must talk."

And he takes off.

All afternoon I'm wondering what he has to talk to me about. Not much seems to upset Dar, but from the sound of his voice, he is seriously freaked out.

After the last bell, Dar pulls me into the stairwell, and he's all out of breath. "Spanky. Before you kill me, here's what happened. Mr. Taylor pulled a bunch of us guys together in the hall," he says, firing words out like a machine gun. "He lectures us about the campout. Again, the whole thing about the rules and the boys' tents and girls' tents."

"Well, duh. Why will I want to kill you about that?"

"Be quiet, Spanky. Just listen to me. He also wanted to know who we were all bunking with. He wanted to know right then and there."

"So what?" I sit down on one of the steps. "We're going to wait it out, so we can get our own tent. . .right?"

Dar leans against the stairwell wall, shaking his head. "Spanky, you're not listening to me. I said he wanted to know right then. So Mack tells Mr. Taylor that I'm bunking with him and Ned."

I jump up, not believing what I'm hearing. "So. You set him straight...right?"

"I didn't know what to say. Mr. Taylor was already writing it down, so I agreed to it on one condition."

"What condition?" I close my eyes. "No, wait. Don't say it. You didn't... Dar?"

"That you'd be in the tent, too."

Chapter 36
Take This the Wrong Way

So that's how Mack, Ned, Dar, and I have become tent mates. It's the morning of the campout. I've gone over my list one last time and I'm ready.

I'm about to turn off my computer when an email pops up from Dad.

"Let's go Spanky," Mom yells from the living room. "If you want me to drive you and your duffle to school, we need to leave right now. Your bag dinner for today is on the counter. And don't forget your jacket. It's a little cool out this afternoon."

"Wait, Mom. I have to read this email from—"

"Print it and take it with you. Let's go!"

I print Dad's email, stick it in my jacket pocket to read on the bus and double check I have his compass in my jeans. Then I load my other jacket pocket with some power bars.

Mom's hands seem shaky on the steering wheel. Maybe I shouldn't be leaving her by herself. What would happen if she puts another towel on the stove? Will she eat anything while I'm gone? If anyone has garbage clogging up their brain, it sure seems like she does.

So I tell her all about what Ms. Badu said. And when we pull into a parking space at school, it's like something magical has happened. Her eyes look . . . I don't know . . . brighter I guess and the air in the car is easier to breathe.

"Garbage? That Ms. Badu has a funny way of putting things," she says. "But from what you just told me, it's like she can read minds."

"Tell me about it, Mom," I say, getting out of the car. "I swear she can see inside my head."

Mom gets out and she's smiling. Really smiling. She gives me the first real hug in weeks. I don't care who sees 'cause now I know I can go on this trip and not worry so much about her. Just by taking out the garbage.

Alice isn't the bus driver so it's a seriously fun bus trip to Apalachuway Park. There's a bunch of adults on board too, but they don't seem to mind everyone talking.

When we get to the camp ground, Mack makes himself real comfortable. He props his backpack against a tree and uses it for a pillow. "Hey, boy scouts," he yells to Dar and me. "You're in the Army now. I'm the general, Ned's the sergeant, and you two are grunts. Set up the tent. And that's an order."

I whisper to Dar, "How much you want to bet he doesn't know how?"

For the rest of the afternoon, Dar and I set up camp. But we follow our own orders. After we find a site high enough that we won't end up in a puddle if it rains, we clear away any rocks or branches and lay a pile of leaves on the ground. Gives it a little cushioning. Then we pitch the tent over the leaves and roll out our sleeping bags inside. Mack and Ned never lift a finger, except to turn the pages of their comic books. When we're done with our tent, we head over to the girl's area to look for Jazz and Maggie.

They're sharing a tent with two other girls and act like they don't want our help. So we kind of watch until they need a hand. They don't. But we help anyway.

Afterwards, all four of us gather wood and kindling and lug it over to where the teachers and chaperones are building what should be a huge campfire. A bunch of kids are sitting around the fire circle.

"I can't wait for the survival training hike," Dar says. "All those Neanderthals that gave us flack about scouting will finally realize how much we know."

Dar reads my mind. Only for me, it's my best chance to impress Jazz.

Mr. Taylor sends all of us back to our tents to grab our bag dinners and when we get back, the campfire is roaring. We're surrounded by tall pines that have to be a zillion years old. I love how they smell. Makes it easier to breathe.

To me, being in the middle of a forest feels just like it used to up north, when you walk outside after a

199

new snowfall. It's so quiet. Sometimes, when I'm in a forest and there's no litter, I pretend I'm the first person who's ever walked there.

But the best part about being in a forest is how many stars you can see. When you get away from the city lights, zillions of them come out of hiding.

Dar and I sit next to each other on one of the long logs surrounding the campfire. We eat our dinners. Stare at the flames. Then Jazz asks Dar if she can sit next to me and I spill my can of soda down the left leg of my jeans.

"Thanks for helping us with our campsite," she says.

"No big deal—" I say, swiping at the soda and then sitting up a little straighter.

"Maybe not to you. But you seem to know a lot more about camping than anyone else around here."

I can't believe it. She noticed! And she's sitting next to me. This can't be happening! Jazz watches the fire. I lean back a little, and watch her.

Suddenly, she looks up. "Will you take a look at Ned? What a lowlife, worming his way next to Maggie. I can't stand that guy. Ned thinks just 'cause he's Mack's buddy and is over at their house all the time that he's Maggie's boyfriend. You'd be my hero if you went over there and sat between her and Ned."

Terrific. Talk about confusing. I have a chance to do something Jazz wants, something she thinks is at least a little heroic, but it means I have to move away from her.

The pines and roaring fire make me feel taller, bolder. So I take the chance. "Actually, I'd really rather hang out with you, Jazz." I hold my breath and wonder if she can hear my heart pounding.

"Look, Spanky," she says. "It's obvious that you like me. I mean, why wouldn't you?" She smiles big time, like she's kidding. "Don't take this the wrong way, but I don't have a lot of time for boys. I'm into my art. Do you understand?"

"Sure," I say, trying not to double over from what feels like a kick in the gut. She sure doesn't seem too busy when it comes to Dar.

"Look. I'm just trying to do you a favor. I don't want you to get mixed up about me."

I hold back the urge to puke. "Nope. I get it." I force a smile. "Thanks for being honest with me. Guess I'll go save Maggie."

I get up and rub my hands on my pants legs, brushing away the dirt and all my hopes.

Chapter 37
Up in Smoke

Maggie is sitting next to another girl on the other side of the fire with her back toward Ned. The two girls' heads are close together and I'm pretty sure they're whispering to each other. I tell Ned some bogus story about Mack looking for him. He gets up, and I take his place. Then I stare at the fire and watch all my Jazz dreams go up in smoke.

"Hi Spanky. Where'd you come from?" Maggie's smile takes a little of the sting out of Jazz dumping me. She hands me a wire hanger opened into a long stick. "Toast a marshmallow?"

Neither of us says anything while our marshmallows turn tan, then brown. Maggie's bursts into flames, so I pull it back, quick, and blow on it as hard as I can.

"Spanky to the rescue," she says.

Campfire flames flicker in her eyes. Sitting here feels cool and weird at the same time—not bad weird, though. Probably smelling the burning wood or toasting marshmallows is melting my brain.

Maggie and I gorge on s'mores and talk about books we like. One of the chaperones has brought a guitar for camp songs. It's the best time I've had since coming to DIP, sitting out here. I've been hoping for Jazz and never really paid much attention to how nice Maggie is. I guess that's what she means by serendipity.

At 9:00, Mr. Taylor halts the sing-along to make some announcements. "Everyone needs to be in their tents by 9:30 p.m. tonight."

We sound like a bunch of moaning coyotes.

"Knock it off. You can use your flashlights in your tents until 10:00, but then lights out! The adults here with us will be out and about, keeping an eye on things. You need to be up at 7 a.m."

"We don't have any alawm clocks," Ned says. "How aw we going to wake up?

Mr. Taylor smiles. "That's my little surprise. You'll find out in the morning. Seriously, guys, get some sleep."

We moan some more.

"I expect you to wash up in the bath house. The building on this side is for boys. The one over there is for the girls. We'll meet in the pavilion at 7:30 a.m. After breakfast, we'll visit the Wild Animal Rehab Grounds— the place they nurse injured animals back to life. I understand you'll be able to hold some of them. If there are any streams here, we'll do some shoreline sampling. I'll tell you more about that at breakfast. After the morning activities, we'll meet back at the pavilion for a weenie roast."

A few kids snicker. Ned elbows Mack who bursts out laughing. Then he covers his crotch with his hand and says, "Not my weenie!"

I barely hold back a giggle. But Maggie shakes her head. "Grow up, Mack," she says, probably to me since Mack and Ned are across the circle and can't hear her. Then she adds, "Do you have any idea what it's like to have a brother like Mack?"

I just shake my head.

Mr. Taylor ignores Mack and keeps on talking. "After lunch, you'll head back to your tents for your compasses. One of the rangers here, Dowl Thompson, is an Eagle Scout, and he'll be teaching you 'orienteering' so you won't get lost during the hike afterwards."

Dar gives me a thumbs-up sign. When Mr. Taylor finishes his announcements, Dar walks around the circle. He looks at Maggie. He looks at me. He raises his eyebrows, and gives me this weird smile. "Ready Romeo?"

"Nite, Spank," says Maggie.

"See ya." My face must be fire red. "Romeo?" I snap, as we head toward our tent. I can't believe the nicknames people want to give me.

Our tent is dark, but we can hear Mack and Ned laughing inside. Dar flips open the front flap and shines his flashlight.

"Turn that thing off!" yells Mack, trying to protect his eyes from the light—eyes that are covered with Dar's night-vision goggles.

I've never seen night vision goggles before. They look a little like binoculars, with a small video-camera-looking piece stuck on to the part that covers your eyes. There's a strap holding the goggles to Mack's head. It runs down from his left ear, cups his chin, up to his right ear, and then over the top of his head,

"Oops. It's four-eyes and his hopeless sidekick," he says, pulling the goggles off. "You don't mind me trying these out, do ya?"

"You could have asked," Dar answers, sounding less upset then I know he must be.

"Oh, quit being such a crybaby," Mack says. "Actually, I did ask."

"It's twue. He did ask," says Ned, slipping into his sleeping bag. "When you didn't say anything, he figawed it was okay." Ned turns on his side and pretends to go to sleep.

"Obviously, I wasn't here to answer you, Mack," says Dar. "I'll take them back now."

"Sure. But I have to go take a leak first. Come on, Ned." Mack pulls the tent flap back.

"Can't Mack. My allawgy pills aw making me sleepy."

"Leave the goggles here, Mack."

But Mack's already outside. Just as quickly, he sticks his head back in, looks at Dar, and says, "Relax

Einstein. You'll get them back when I'm good and ready."

The tent flap slaps closed. The sound of leaves crunching gets softer as he walks away. Then it gets loud again and the tent flap swings open.

The Zisenell NVG9 Vipers are propped above his eyes, but not covering them. "If I'm not in my sleeping bag in ten minutes," he says, "call for backup."

We decide Mack is sneaking around the campsite, trying to scare everyone in their tents. I turn my flashlight back on. "How about them having an eagle scout here?"

Dar smiles. "If kids only knew what it took to earn Eagle. No one would ever kid a scout again."

Our tent muffles the sound of kids shouting and laughing while the chaperones are telling them to knock it off.

"LIGHTS OUT!"

Dar closes the empty case for his night vision goggles. He slips into his sleeping bag, and mutters, "I hope he gets lost. Good night."

"Seriously." After I say it, I suddenly realize I don't mean it. It makes no sense. I don't care two beans about Mack. But I can't stop wondering where he is and why he hasn't come back.

Dar's breathing tells me he's fallen asleep. Then I hear leaf crunches and figure Mack is back. Only when the flap lifts up, it's Mr. Taylor, pointing his flashlight around the tent. He calls out to someone behind him, "Spanky, Dar, Ned. . .where's Mack?"

"He went to the outhouse," I say, and roll over like I'm going to sleep.

"I have more tents to check. But I'll be back in five. He'd better be here."

I sit up for a while, waiting and listening. Ned hasn't moved a finger since Mack took off. Guess his allergy pills knocked him out cold.

The smell of mold makes me wonder how long it's been since anyone has used our tent. My eyes adjust to the darkness and as I stare at Mack's untouched bed roll, my legs feel like they're filled with jumping beans. I should be hoping he falls off a cliff, if there were cliffs in Florida. Instead, I imagine him quietly hiding behind trees, or acting like a stealth bomber, pretending he's on some mission far away from his dad. Mack sure doesn't need any more trouble. His dad will probably kill him. But why should I care?

It's hard to explain why you do something you know is wrong. Maybe it's like Dad said. *Sometimes we're doing the wrong things for the right reason.* Maybe my reason is a good one. Deep down, I know it won't make up for what I'm about to do. I roll out Mack's sleeping bag, and wad up my extra clothes to look like a body is inside. And I pretend to sleep.

Ten minutes later, the flap moves and Taylor says to someone, "That's all of them. Let's hit the sack. Who's on watch for the next hour?"

Chapter 38
What Was That?

I shake Dar. "Wake up."

"Huh...?"

"Wake up! Mack never came back. We've got to go look for him."

Dar throws open his bag. "And why should I care? Go back to sleep!" He yanks the top cover back over his head.

My gut feels like it's full of worms. "We have to find him. C'mon, Dar. Don't make me go alone."

"What part of 'go back to sleep' don't you understand?" Dar's sleeping bag muffles his voice.

I put on my shoes and jacket and slip my head out of the tent flap, looking for chaperones on watch. I see one, but quietly head out and hide behind a tree. I can barely see two feet in front of me, but I don't want to turn on my flashlight until I'm far enough away from the other tents. Might as well try the bathhouse. At least it's lit.

Someone is behind me. "Wait."

Dar. I motion for him to be quiet and wait 'til he catches up.

We move from tree to tree. Dar's actually pretty light on his feet, skinny as he is "What's with you anyway, Spanky," he says. "Why should we care about what Mack's doing?"

Nothing I can say will make sense. "Don't you care about getting your night-vision goggles back?"

Dar picks up his pace. "And how do you propose we find him?"

"He said he had to take a pee. We'll start at the bath house. Even if he can see in the dark, I bet he'll want to keep the light from that building in range."

"Good point."

We check all the stalls in the bathhouse and whisper, "Mack? Are you here?" But the place is empty. One of the chaperones comes in as we head back outside.

"G'nite," we say. We hear the sound of water running inside. Staying in the shadows of the building, we try to figure out which direction Mack might have taken. Dar slips back to the entrance to the men's outhouse, spins around, and starts walking in a straight path towards the woods. "Come on," he says. "This is as good a direction as any."

"Hold up," I say, starting to have some doubts. "Maybe we should tell Mr. Taylor Mack's missing."

"Oh. So now you want to do the right thing. Why didn't you just do that to begin with? Instead of waking me up?"

I've never been able to get the picture of Mack's dad holding him by the collar and shaking him. "So kill me. But something isn't right. Mack could be in trouble. He'll be expelled if Taylor knows he's out wandering around."

"As will we!"

"We'll find him and get him back in the tent before anyone knows we're missing. Just wait here for a second. I'm going to tell Ned that if we're not back in an hour, to tell Mr. Taylor."

Tree to tree, I sneak back to our tent, wake Ned and tell him what's up. But his eyes keep closing. "C'mon Ned. Wake up!" I shake him. "You need to stay awake. If we're not back in an hour, tell Mr. Taylor that the three of us left to try out Dar's night vision goggles. But we never came back. Can you do that?"

"I want to go with you," he says, rubbing his eyes.

"No Ned. You have to stay here...just in case."

"Okeedokee. I'll tell Taylaw you guys went home," Ned says, and rolls over.

"No. Don't you dare tell him we went home! You need to tell Mr. Taylor to come—"

But Ned's already snoring. Some good he'll be.

When I find Dar, I pull Dad's compass out of my pocket and check the florescent face—our heading is due north. My Orienteering badge is about to come in handy. Estimating the length of two long steps to be about five feet, I start counting. Five...ten...fifteen...

We walk silently, our flashlights blazing a path. The smell of burning wood and smoke from the campfire hangs in the air.

Crack!

We freeze. "What was that?"

Dar shrugs. I try to quiet my breathing.

"Maybe an animal," he says, crouching down. "Or maybe Mack?"

My knees hit the ground and we wait, hoping to hear other sounds. This is no night to be lost in the woods. A pitch black blanket has covered everything and the moon's as thin as a frown. Only the two spots from our flashlights and the faint light behind us break the darkness.

Then I hear a strange sound. Maybe a moan. Really faint though.

"Did you hear that?" I ask, my heartbeat kicking up a notch.

"That has to be Mack. The intelligent thing to do is to retrace our steps and tell Mr. Taylor," Dar says.

"Darn it, Dar, we can hear him. Right? All we have to do is get to him, and bring him back to the tent."

Neither of us says anything until we hear the moaning sound again. Dar shakes his head and stands up. "I can't believe I let you get me into this."

The worry in Dar's voice tells me he's thinking the same thing I am. There's no turning back now.

Chapter 39
Bombs Away

I check my compass again. We bolt in the direction of the cry—20 degrees west of due north. Again, I count my steps. Five, ten, fifteen, twenty...forty...eighty...one hundred. We stop and crouch down again.

Everything is so still. "Mack?" I whisper-yell through the trees.

Whoo? Whoo? Only some 'ole owl responds.

My breath is gasping in and out, and my pulse is pounding in my ears.

Then, from somewhere even deeper in the woods, we hear Mack loud and clear. "Help me."

I look back in the direction of the bath house to get my bearings. The faint light has disappeared. All I can see are the outlines of trees. And they all look alike.

"We're totally lost now," Dar says. "How are we going to get help?"

"No we're not!" I recite our steps to myself. "I've got my compass. I've been counting our paces. We're cool, Dar."

"Someone. Help me."

We start fast-walking toward his voice. I aim my flashlight ahead. More trees. I move the beam of light left, then right. Nothing but a sign. "DANGER! NO TRESPASSING! DANGER!"

We freeze.

"Terrific. As if we need a sign to tell us it's dangerous out here."

"We've probably left the park and are entering someone's land," Dar says, barely loud enough for me to hear. "Sometimes people put up signs like this just to scare people off."

Dar's explanation settles me down. I bend over, trying to catch my breath. "Mack? Where are you?"

"D-d-down here."

Mack's voice is coming from the ground, about twenty feet ahead. Did he trip and sprain an ankle? I fan the area with my flashlight. The beam bounces off nearby trees. Directly in front of us, there's a barbed wire fence, partly upright but mostly fallen over. Beyond the fence, total darkness.

Dar calls out. "Mack! Talk to us so we can find you."

No response.

"Mack?"

"Down here, you morons!" His voice is coming from the ground—more like from under the ground.

We step over the opening in the barbed fence. A spot of flashlight skips ten feet ahead. The ground disappears into nothingness.

"It's a sinkhole!" Dar cries.

"Whoa. Check that out."

It's like the ground just collapsed. Dozens of trees look like pick-up sticks. Some are toppled over. Others look like their roots pulled them straight down when the ground gave way.

There's this spider web of leaves, moss, and tree limbs. And there's Mack. He's lying on top of the web about twelve feet down.

Dar's flashlight spot circles the hole.

"Idiots. Don't shine your flashlight at me," yells Mack.

"Oh right," says Dar. "The goggles. The light is blinding him. Spanky. We could be standing on top of huge caverns!"

I step back. "What?"

"With all this weather change, I bet it's a new sink hole. Groundwater dissolves underground rocks and makes caverns. If they get too big and can't hold up the surface, bombs away!"

I couldn't believe we almost walked right into it. "Seriously?" I drop down near the edge but a couple feet back for safety.

Dar kneels next to me, and yells, "Mack. We're up here. What happened?"

"I fell in this freakin' hole. I can't get out...I...I think I broke my leg."

"Who's the moron now, Malone?" yells Dar.

There's a thud under us. And a vibration. Dar and I look at each other. And we both know it's that split second, that moment right before you know something is about to go very wrong.

"Ohhhhh craaaaaaaaaap!"

Chapter 40
I Can't Breathe!

The edge of the sinkhole gives way. We tumble forward, falling head first into the darkness below.

Arms flailing. Screaming. Somersaulting. Falling. Ahhhhh! Dirt. Uuchhh.

BAM!

"Spanky. Where are you? Spanky!"

Spanky? My name is Spanky. I'm Spanky.

"Spanky. Talk to me. Are you okay?"

Open your eyes. Am I dead? Can't move.

"SPANKY! TALK TO ME!"

Dar. That's Dar. Flex fingers. Where am I? Rough bark. A tree. I'm on a tree. The trunk. I'm half on the trunk and half off it. Pain. Sharp pain. My head. Hurts bad. Dirt...something wet in my mouth.

"Spanky? Is that you?"

I'm not dead am I? No. I'm not dead. Speak. Say something. "I'm...I'm down here. Okay. I'm okay. Where are you?"

"Over here." Dar's voice is coming from my left, about five feet away. "I must have slipped through some branches. My wrist hurts. Lost my flashlight. It's amazingly dark down here. I can't see my hand in front of my face. No. NO! My glasses. They're gone!"

Suddenly, I remember why we fell in this hole in the first place. "Mack. Where are you?" No reply.

"Mack! Come on, man. Talk to me!"

Dar chimes in. "Mack where are you?"

Something's pushing at my ankle. I freak and jerk my leg away. What the heck is that?

A muffled voice rises from under me. "Get off me, Spanky." It's Mack. "Your foot's on top of my face," he moans. "I can't breathe."

Afraid of falling further, I don't move. But I have to get off of Mack. Slowly, I pull myself all the way onto the trunk, hugging it with my arms and legs.

Shhhwuump!

Oh jeez. Oh jeez. Oh jeez! The trunk drops and immediately jolts to a stop.

"Ohhhhhh!" Mack sounds like he's crying.

My heart's hammering away. I wait. But nothing else happens. "Mack. I can hear you but I can't see you. Are you still wearing the goggles? Am I off you?"

217

"Yeah. Oh man. You gotta help me. Please. Help me. I think I broke my leg. I can't move."

Mack sounds bad. How the heck am I going to move him myself? And even if I can, where can I move him to? I'll need Dar's help. But being trapped under branches, he's useless. I start shaking, bad.

NO! I scream silently. You can't freeze now.

Chapter 41
Everything is Green

If I don't calm down, I could end up killing all three of us. If only I could see better. "Mack, can you give me the goggles?" I say, trying not to make any big moves.

"Yeah, yeah. I can see you. Oh man. It hurts. Hurts so bad."

I can't see Mack, but the sound of his voice is coming from behind and below me. "What hurts? Is it just your leg?"

"Yeah. Shut up and listen. Dar's close to the rim, six feet, front of you. I'm, I'm, couple feet behind you, behind you, to your left. You. You're on a tree trunk. On its side. Wedged between the sides of the hole. Branches are holding us up."

I'll be better off spinning my body around to get closer to Mack. But that means I have to quit hugging the tree. Don't think about it. Just do it. Carefully. Spin round, like a wheel.

"You're almost facing me," says Mack.

I hug the trunk again. "Mack, hand me the goggles."

"Okay. I think... I can move them along the trunk. Toward you. Ouch, ouch!! Ahhh!"

"What's wrong Mack? Talk to me."

"I can't . . .can't move very far. It hurts. Oh jeez, it hurts so much. Come on, man. Help me."

"Mack, I want you to just set the goggles up on the trunk, but hold on to them. Whatever you do, don't let go of them."

Mack grunts and scrapes the trunk with the goggles. Like a blind guy, I feel around in the darkness. I inch forward and stretch my arm toward Mack's voice. I feel the rubbery strap. "Got 'em. Dar? Where are you?"

"Beneath some branches. My wrist is throbbing. Any chance you can help me, too?"

I try pulling the goggles over my head, but I can't get the straps right without losing my balance. They're pretty darn heavy. I can only get them half way on. So I lay flat on the trunk, hold on with one arm, and use my other hand to get them in position.

Which way do these straps go—oh my God. This is amazing! Everything is green. Eerie green. It's like I'm looking down a tunnel. I have to turn my head to see stuff I'd normally see out of the sides of my eyes. From the sound of Mack's voice, he seems so close to me. But through the glasses he looks far away. Maybe that's how he fell in this hole. Maybe it looked further away than it was.

"Whoa! Night-vision things are beyond cool. I can see you guys. But everything is green. Whatever you do, don't move. I think you're right Mack. The branches are stopping us from falling deeper. I don't know how deep this hole is, but we could be in big trouble if these branches give way."

Chapter 42
I'm Going to Die

"Do something. I'm gonna die."

"Hang in there Mack. You're not going to die. It's your right leg that hurts?"

"Yeah, why?"

"There's a huge rock on it is why. The web of branches is holding it up, I guess."

"I know. Hurts. So bad."

I get as close as I can. The boulder is pressing on the top of his knee. His jeans look darker in one spot near the boulder. Has to be blood. Doesn't look like a lot though. "Mack, listen to me. You're not going to die."

"Spanky," says Dar. "Pull me out of here so I can help you."

"Can you move? You're under some branches, but it looks like you can slide out to your left. No wait. Don't move. I see your glasses. If you move, you might knock them into the hole."

I spit out some more dirt and drag my tongue across my sleeve to get rid of a weird taste in my mouth. Instead of spinning my body back around again, I scoot backwards along the trunk until I reach the side where Dar lies trapped. His glasses are sticking out of some loose dirt that must have fallen in when we fell. I grab them. "Dar, which wrist hurts?"

"My right one."

"Put your left hand out toward me. Good. Here's your glasses. Now give me your left arm again. I'm going to grab it and pull you. But we gotta take it slow. Ease yourself out."

Dar holds my arm. As I pull him out from under the branches, he frantically moves his bad hand up, down, sideways, trying to find something to grab. "Ah, crap," he cries. "I can't hold on. My wrist is killing me."

More dirt slides down the side of the hole.

"Dar, there's a thick branch under you. Put one of your feet down to the left. I think it can hold you until I can pull you up on this trunk. Test it first. And be careful."

Crack!

"HELP!" Dar's body slips down a foot.

He must have stepped on a different branch. My heart is doing back flips. I feel like I'm falling, too. Only I'm still hugging the trunk that doesn't seem to be going anywhere. STOP IT. Stop freaking out. Just stop and THINK!

"Dar. It's going to be ok. What are the odds that I'd find your glasses?"

223

"Pure luck. We're doomed."

"We're going to be ok. I'm going to try to pull you up and over this trunk." It's now or never. I unwrap my legs and turn sideways so only the top half of me is on the trunk. I wedge my feet into the web of branches behind me for support and lean over the trunk. Then I stretch my arm as far as it will go toward Dar.

"NOW, DAR! Give me your arm!" I grab it and pull with all my might. Lucky for me, Dar "the human straw" doesn't weigh all that much. As soon as I get him moving, he lets go of me and pulls with his good arm. I grab his waistband and help him over the trunk. My chest hurts from breathing so hard. "I . . . I . . .think this should hold us."

"My wrist is useless," says Dar. "This is petrifying, but I suppose I'll be okay."

I know now that I'm on my own getting Mack out. Heck, getting all of us out of here. Maybe Ned's talking to Mr. Taylor. We've been gone for at least an hour. A search party could be on the way. "Dar, I think we should yell for help. Maybe someone will hear us. Come on. On the count of three. Ready? One, two, three ...HEEEEEEEELLLLLLLLLLLLLLLP!"

No one answers.

We try again and again. Nothing. The silence squeezes my chest.

I have to keep reminding myself that one wrong move and the sinkhole could give way even more. I turn back toward Mack, but now I feel woozy. My head hurts. Something is dripping down my chin. Probably tree sap.

I slide the few inches toward Mack. To his right, just past the boulder, there's an opening in the tree's webbed branches. "Mack. To your right. Do you see that hole?"

"Wait," yells Dar. "Mack. Don't move. Oh, man this hurts. I've got my flashlight." Dar moves the light back and forth across Mack until he finds the hole.

"Turn that off." Now I see what Dar was talking about. With the goggles on, his flashlight blinds me.

"Yep. I s . . . s . . . see . . . the hole," says Mack. "You're going to push me down it, aren't you?"

"Huh? Just shut up and let me figure this out."

If the branches are strong enough to hold up that boulder, I figure Mack's okay. He'll feel better if I can get the boulder away from his leg. If I can get it to fall down the hole, all the better.

"Grab on to the branches, Mack," I say as calmly as I can. "I'm going to use my feet as a lever to push that boulder off your leg toward that hole."

"It's going to hurt so bad."

"You can do this," I say, trying to keep my voice steady, wondering if I'm talking to myself or to Mack. But what if he goes down the hole instead of the boulder? No way. The branches are too thick. STOP IT. I go over my plan. I've made a decision. Now I just have to do it!

Still on my stomach, I spin sideways so my feet will be near the bolder. Knees bent, I edge my feet backwards so they barely touch it.

"Okay Mack, here we go. When I say three, I'm going to shove that boulder as hard as I can away from you. When I do, hold on to the branches, but try to move your bad leg toward me. It's going to hurt, Mack, but you're tough. You can handle it. It's the only way."

I close my eyes as tight as I can, take a deep breath, and clench my jaw. "One...two...three. Now, Mack. Now!

"Ahhhhhhhhhhh!"

Chapter 43
We're Going to Die

The trees groan, but the boulder doesn't move. It weighs a lot more than I expected. I take another deep breath and force every last bit of energy I have through my feet.

It moves. I mean, not like Superman could have moved it. But it moves just enough to free Mack's leg. The branches groan again, but don't move.

"How ya doin, Mack?" I call, starting to shake again. "T-t-t-alk to me."

"Don't know. Better. My l-leg. Spanky...."

I wait for my shakes to stop. "Breathe, Mack. Take a deep breath. You're going to be okay. We're going to get out of here. I promise."

"S-s-sure we are."

"Let's call for help again. Together now, on three. One, two, three, HELLLLLLLLLP!" Our cries for help sound muffled as if the three of us are lying in an airtight box.

Mack keeps screaming on his own. "HELLLLP! HELLP! HELLLLLLLP!"

"Mack's panicking. Could go into shock, too, Spank," Dar says.

"HELLLLLLLLP! HELLLLLLP! HELP! HELP! HELLLLLP!"

Tough guy Mack who sees himself as an Army General is screaming for dear life. Wait. That's it.

As loud and commanding as I can, I yell, "At ease, soldier!"

"HELLLP. Hellllp. Help . . ." Mack's voice gets quieter.

"At ease, Mack. We're in enemy territory."

"Huh?"

"There's danger below us. We need to stay as still as possible."

"Oh. Man. Ss-s-cared."

Dar yells, "We must conserve our energy, soldier."

He's right about that. "It's cool Mack. In the morning, when everyone goes to the bath house, someone will hear us. We just need to get through the night."

The three of us don't say anything else for a long while. The wind picks up. The trees that are still standing sway. Then nothing. Silence. Like a wet cloud is hanging over us. Suddenly the wind kicks up again, whistling through the leaves.

Mack breaks the silence. He's sounding like his old self again. "Swear on my mother's grave."

"What's that, Mack?" I ask.

228

"Don't tell anyone I was crying. Swear to it."

"It's okay, man."

Mack's stomach makes a noise and we all laugh. "Guess I'm hungry," he says. "While you guys were eating dinner around the campfire, me and Ned left. Played with the night vision goggles."

He's starting to sound better. I remember my power bars. "Hang on." I feel around in my jacket pocket. "I've got something. Here Mack. Dar, you can have the other one."

"What about you?" Dar asks.

"It's okay. I'm still full from eating marshmallows with Maggie." As soon as her name rolls out of my mouth, I wish I'd never said it.

"Did you just say Maggie? As in, my sister Maggie?" Mack's voice is quiet. "Maggie and McDork?" Then Mack starts singing in a strained voice, "Spanky and Maggie, sit. . .sitting in a tree. K...K...K-I-S-S-I-N-G..." The old Mack is definitely back.

"Shut up, Mack!" Dar yells.

But Mack's singing relieves me. "Mack's on to something," I say, and burst out laughing. "But he doesn't have the words right. He should be singing, 'Spanky, Mack and Dar, sitting in a bunch of trees." The next thing I know, we're all laughing. Laughing like a bunch of monkeys. Then Shwwoomp! We drop, about a foot.

Mack starts sobbing. "We're never getting out of here. We're going to die."

Chapter 44
I Couldn't Stop Crying

"I'm going to take care of you, Mack," I say. "I can't get us out of here tonight, but we're going to be fine. Trust me, Mack. I'm right here."

"Of course you're right there, you little butt-wipe. No. Wait. I didn't mean that. You're trying to save my life."

"Forget about it." Hearing Mack apologize gets me worried again. Maybe he's not okay. "Relax, Mack. Everything's going to be fine. I swear on your mother's grave."

"You can't say anything," Mack says. "About me crying. And everything's not fine."

Mack's sobbing. Seriously sobbing. "It's okay to cry, Mack," I say. "You're in pain, for crying out loud."

But it's like he doesn't hear me when he says, "The last time...when my mom...when my mom. . ."

"When your mom what?" snaps Dar. Through the goggles, I see him unwrapping his power bar.

"You guys promise. Swear you'll never say anything about me being scared or crying. Swear!" says Mack.

"Forget about it," I say. "It's not like Dar and I haven't cried before. Right, Dar?"

"On occasion. What's the big deal?"

"What's the big deal? I'll tell you dweebs what's the big deal. You have moms. But mine—she was, she was in . . . she was in . . ."

I'm glad Mack can't see Dar roll his eyes. I know what it's like to be tripped up in your thoughts. "It's okay, Mack. Your Mom. She was where?"

"In a hospital bed. There were tubes and wires coming out of her. I couldn't help it. . ."

"It wasn't exactly your fault," says Dar.

"My fault? Of course it wasn't my fault, brainiac. I was a little kid. I was scared. I tried, but I couldn't stop crying."

I have to calm Mack down. If he gets more upset, he could do something that kills all of us. "Why do you think you shouldn't have cried?" I whisper. "I'd have cried too. Who wouldn't have?"

"My older brothers. That's who," Mack yells. "My two perfect brothers who never do anything wrong! They just stood there like two statues. Thinking they're so tough and brave. Dad didn't care if Maggie cried, but he grabbed me by my shoulders and said, 'You get a hold of yourself and quit this baby crap. Be brave like your two brothers.'"

Mack is now shouting his story. "Then he pulled me into the hall and slapped me hard. Only I couldn't stop crying. I didn't want to stop crying. I was so mad at him and at my brothers 'cause they acted like they didn't care. I swore I'd never be like them."

"Sure, Mack," I say, hoping to get Mack to chill out. "Who would blame you? It's okay. Seriously."

It was like Dad used to say about it getting calm after a storm. Mack shut up. All that stuff exploded right out of him. I guess he finally took out the garbage.

Now everything is still. Too still. Eerie still. Then a pine cone falls. Or an animal creeps through the leaves. We're sure every noise is a gator or a snake.

Chapter 45
It Doesn't Look Like a Widow

Mack exploding about his mother makes me see how dumb I've been not to tell anyone about my dad. Or my mom for that matter. I mean, in a way, I get Mack. This gives me an idea.

"We gotta get through the night. So how about we kill some time and play 'Truth or Dare.' But . . . I'm thinking we keep it to just truths. We've had enough daring for the night. Mack, you've already given up a major truth, you get to ask the first question."

He doesn't say anything at first. "Ummmph. I don't. . .Ok. McDoog, what's the strangest thing that's ever happened to you."

"The strangest thing that ever happened to me?" I repeat his question to get up the nerve to tell the truth. Oh what the heck. "Since my dad left. I keep freaking out. Like when Dar and I were trying to give Miss A CPR and I froze."

Dar says, "Well you sure didn't freak out tonight. You're the only calm one here."

"I guess I've been holding too much garbage in my head."

Mack actually laughs. "Garbage? What the heck are you talking about?"

"Well, it's a no wonder," says Dar. "With your dad serving in Afghanistan and—"

"What?" Mack yells. "Your dad's a soldier and you never told me?"

"Well, we haven't exactly been friends, Mack." I get that bad taste in my mouth again.

The night-vision goggles are amazing. I see a spider crawl on Mack's head. It doesn't look like a widow. More like a daddy longlegs. But before I can tell him, he slaps it, then shakes his head from side to side. I check his leg again. The dark stain looks the same. Remembering my real first aid training, I'm thinking he won't need a tourniquet.

Mack blurts out, "Come to think of it, I had something weird happen to me in school."

"What?" asks Dar.

"Nothing." He scrunches his face up. I thought maybe he was feeling better. Guess not.

"Come on, Mack," says Dar. "We're going to be here for a long time. Tell us."

"Spanky already knows about it from me telling Ned. And I've changed my mind."

So Dar tells me to ask a question.

"Might as well ask you too, Dar. What's your strangest experience?"

He tells Mack about my dream and Ms. Badu humming Glory Hallelujah and how she hummed the same song the next day in class. He tells Mack how I was beginning to think Ms. Badu was a witch.

"For a split second," says Dar, "I thought the same thing." Now Dar's laughing so hard, I think the trees are going to move. "Ms. Badu a witch. And I actually thought the same thing? Can you believe that? Now that's strange!"

Then Dar says. "Mack, remember that day when you were the teacher? You actually sounded smart for once."

Mack says, "Yeah. That's what I was going to . . .it had to have been Ms. Badu's purple marker. It turned me into . . . you!"

Still holding tight to the trunk we're both sitting on, Dar lets go with his bad hand to cover a yawn. "The purple marker? No way. You obviously have some intelligence. If Ms. Badu had anything to do with it, she just helped you relax and you forgot to play dumb."

"Yeah, right, four eyes. You sound just like my teachers. They always say that I used to be smart before I stopped trying. Nah . . . it had to have been that marker."

Now I'm curious. "Why'd you stop trying?"

"I just told you, you little butt—I mean, sorry. I didn't want to be like my brothers. If they were going to be perfect Boy Scouts and get straight A's, I was going to do just the opposite."

"How's that working for you?"

"I end up in Blowfish's stinky pit every day, and my dad is always beating on me. My only friend is Ned. He's okay, but I guess it makes me a loser, having only one friend."

I know exactly what he means.

Then Mack asks, "Spanky, if you could be anyone else in the world for one day, who would you be?"

Wow. A name comes into my head almost immediately. Not one I expected. "I'd like to be you for a day, Mack."

Dar says, "Excuse me?"

"Riiiiight," Mack says.

"Here's the thing. You say whatever you want. You do whatever you want. My brain and my body have been having a hard time talking to each other so I end up doing nothing. For one day, I'd like to do everything I want."

"That's a laugh," Mack says. "At least you use your brain. And you may have saved my life. If we ever get out of here, that is."

"Whatever. I just wish I had your guts."

Mack's eyes stare off at something none of us can see. He shakes his head. "What I've been doing doesn't take guts. But what you did tonight—

He doesn't finish his sentence. It's quiet for a while

Then, as if we've read each other's minds, at the exact same time, Mack and I say, "Who'd you like to be, Dar?"

Through the goggles, I see Dar smiling. He says, "Spanky, take those glasses off for a second." After I do, he puts the flashlight under his chin, shining up so his face looks spooky.

"Einstein."

***

Somehow, between long silences, and playing more Truth, hours pass. Dar's wrist still hurts, but I help him spin around on the trunk and move closer to a Y-shaped branch that holds him for the night. I ease closer to Mack and drape my jacket over him. After a few minutes, I think he's gone to sleep.

Dar whispers, "Do you think Mack's okay?"

Mack's eyes pop open. I figure he wants to hear what I'll say.

"Malone's a tough soldier. He can handle this."

Mack smiles, then closes his eyes.

I'm not sure if any of us are sleeping for more than a few seconds at a time. Any slight movement jolts us awake. Sometimes it's from below. Then it's the rustle of the wind through the leaves above us.

I sling the goggle strap over my shoulder and tell myself it's just one night. Anyone can get through one short night.

Chapter 46
Red, Black and Yellow

"SPANKY!"

My body jerks, but in place, as if it knows not to move too far. The sky has changed from black to grey. We've made it to morning. "Yeah. What?"

"Shhhh. Snake. Behind you. In the tree. Over Dar."

I want to turn around to see what it looks like, but I know not to make any moves. I whisper, "What kind?"

"How would I know what kind of snake it is? Dar, wake up."

I keep my voice soft, but intense at the same time. "Shut up, Mack. He's better off asleep. Tell me what it looks like."

"Too late," whispers Mack. "Dar. Don't move. There's a snake on the limb of a tree to your right. About ten feet up."

I whisper, "Dar. Don't move your body. Don't even move your eyes. Pretend like you're dead."

"It's moving its tail. Do you hear any sound?" Mack asks. "Oh crap! What if it's a rattler?"

That scares me. Big time. I haven't seen any water. Probably isn't a cottonmouth or a copperhead. Have to rule out a diamondback. It could be one in these woods. Rattles its tail. Seriously venomous. Seriously dangerous. "Mack, does it have diamonds on its back?"

"No diamonds."

I let my breath out slowly. "What color is it?"

"It's red, black and yellow," whispers Mack.

"Does it—"

"Maybe not yellow. The yellow could be orange and the red could be brown. I'm a little color blind."

"Great." I replay Dad's jingle. But if Mack can't tell colors, it's useless.

I'm getting shaky. Keep it together. You know this stuff! "Does it have rings around its body or any stripes?"

"It's definitely not striped. More splotchy, if you ask me. But I'm definitely not sure about the color. The yellow could be orange or heck, I don't know. Could be gray."

"Spanky. Identify the snake!" whispers Dar. "Tell me it's not poisonous."

"Pretend you're dead, Dar. Mack, you said it was splotchy. Is there a dark outline to the splotches?"

"Yeah. Yeah. What's that mean?"

Knowing Mack is colorblind, I don't know what to think. If he's orange and splotchy, he probably isn't dangerous. But if he's really gray with splotches, it could be a Dusky Pygmy. The rattlesnake that bites more people in Florida than any other snake.

Chapter 47
We're in This Together

So so so slowly, I ease my head around to look. And then I know. I've seen that snake before.

"It's a corn snake. It eats stuff like rats and birds. Don't make any quick moves though. Could freak him out. But he's not poisonous."

"You're sure?" Dar asks, sounding freaked out.

"Yeah. My cousin has one for a pet. Calls him Watson. Raised him since he was a little thing."

"So if it's a pet kind of snake, what's it doing out here?"

"Corn snakes live in the wild, too." I say, and realize Mack's staring at me with this strange look on his face. "You okay?" I ask.

But Mack keeps staring at me, and says, "Are YOU okay?"

"I'm fine, Mack. Just hang in there."

We watch and wait. Finally, the bright curve of the sun makes it above the horizon and the snake finally slides away.

Dah DAH DI di dah, dah DAH DI di dah

"It's a bugle," I shout. "Mr. Taylor's surprise was to wake us up!" I'm excited. That means the kids will be getting up.

"They're playing "Reveille," says Mack. "It's the bugle call the army uses to wake up soldiers."

Both Dar and I know that, but we look at each other and just say, "Cool!"

Muffled sounds are coming from the campground.

"We're going to be saved!" Mack says.

"Unless Ned told Mr. Taylor we've gone home," I say, and for a second, a wave of panic comes over me. Then I realize how stupid that sounds. "Oh jeez. As if Taylor would ever believe that. Dar, Mack. We have to yell so they hear us." And we start yelling. Soon enough, we hear kids and adults calling our names. We holler some more. It takes forever but they find us.

***

"Stay back here!"

I can't believe how happy I am to hear Mr. Taylor's voice.

"Is that you, Mack? You weally fweaked us out. What are you doing in this hole?"

"Ned!" Taylor yells. "Get back here. I told you to stay back there with the others."

I follow the crunching sound of Taylors' shoes on leaves above us as he walks around the hole. He's smart enough to find a solid spot on the other side.

"Boys, talk to me," he says. "Is anyone hurt?"

I yell, "Dar and I are okay. Mack's pretty bad off."

Mr. Taylor pulls out his cell phone and calls 911. A long while later, maybe a half-hour or so, a forest ranger and some firemen arrive. They spend a lot of time finding a good spot to set up their ropes. Two firemen at the top lower another guy in a harness. He uses his feet to ease himself down the side. He tells Dar to hold on to him and the other guys pulls both of them out.

Another fireman asks me if I can scoot back along the trunk to the side where Dar has been. "Sure thing," I say. "Did it a couple times last night. But Mack should go first. He's hurting bad."

"No son. I want you, first," he replies, in a voice that sounds like my dad when he's trying to be nice, but letting me know he means business. "We're going to need other equipment to get your friend out."

They lower the first fireman down again. I inch my way back. When I look behind me, he's staring at my hair. "Hey kid. What's your name?

"Spanky."

"What day is it?"

"Sunday. Why?"

He ignores my question. "Let's get you out of here. Hold on to my arm to turn around. Then put your arms around my neck and your legs around my waist."

As the guy at the top pulls, he carefully eases us up the side.

From above, the sinkhole looks even deeper than we imagined. You can kind of see between some of the trees. I guess the tree roots saved us. Mr. Taylor is keeping the kids back on the other side of the sinkhole. But they're staring at me with strange looks on their faces.

"We could have fallen a lot further," I say to the fireman who brought me up.

"It was night. There was no way of knowing," he says, forcing me to move back from the edge. "You did the right thing by staying put until morning. Besides, this sinkhole could grow deeper still. Hard to say. We have to be extremely careful. Now let's take a look at your head."

"What's wrong with my head?"

He wipes my hair with some liquid. Stings like crazy. But I'm more interested in watching them save Mack.

The guy rescuing him lays the stretcher on the web and puts a splint on Mack's leg. Now the guys up top are pulling him out. The fireman below keeps adjusting the halter of ropes so Mack's lying flat.

Poor Mack is moaning big time. I don't want him seeing me stare at him so I turn away. I also don't want to watch if they drop him.

Within a couple minutes, both Mack and the fireman are above ground. I feel a tap on my shoulder.

"Spanky, oh my gosh! Are you all right?" It's Maggie.

I turn around as Jazz chimes in, "Yeah, you don't look so good. You okay?"

Weird. I'm happier to see Maggie. I guess s'mores'll do that to you.

Dar shows us the splint a medic put on his wrist, then joins the others in staring at my head. "I'm glad I was behind you down there," he says. "Your head—"

"You both okay?" Mr. Taylor walks up. He checks out my head too, but just smiles and puts his arms around Dar's and my shoulders.

There's a commotion as a couple firemen move Mack's stretcher and set it down a few feet from us.

Mr. Taylor looks at Mack. "Mack, you look like you're in a lot of pain."

Mack's eyes look like my mom's did the day she found out Dad was leaving. Dark. Kind of sunken. Tired. I even think he looks a little scared. Lost. He knows he's in trouble.

Taylor says, "My guess is, you were behind this fiasco."

I step in between him and Mack. "Mr. Taylor. It wasn't all Mack's fault. None of us should have been out in the woods after lights out. It's just that we were all interested in trying out the night-vision goggles. Dar and I fell into the sinkhole the same way Mack did."

Okay, so maybe I'm leaving out some important details. But what I said wasn't a lie. Mack looks at me, I look at Dar, and Dar looks at Mack. We are in this together.

Chapter 48
Blood Brothers

Secretly, I hoped for flashing lights and blaring sirens on the way to the hospital. But no such luck. I search for another power bar. My fingers touch paper and I can't believe I'd forgotten all about Dad's letter.

Spanky:

I met Rasheed and his family again yesterday afternoon. With the help of an interpreter, I told him all about you and that we'd just moved to Appalacheeville when I left for Afghanistan.

He looked surprised when I said you called him Mr. Powerful, and that you were sorry he'd lost his house.

Here's what he said. "Even though I must now live in a tent instead of my house, I have both of my parents close by to look after me. Tell your son I'm sorry that his father has to be so far away. Tell him that I should be calling him Mr. Powerful."

Spanky, it took Rasheed's comment to help me see how hard this must be for you. I'd been so worried about the house and Mom, I didn't spend enough time thinking about you and what it would be like starting a new school in a new town and taking care of everything on your own, with me far away. I'm sorry, pal.

Let me hear about your camping trip when you get back. Have you figured out anything about that guy, Mack?

Love, Dad

P.S. Mom tells me you've been keeping up with the chores, cheering her up, and handling your school work. You're doing everything I expected from you. No soldier could be prouder than I am to have you for a son!

* * *

It's our first day back. On our way up the stairs, Dar says, "I can't believe how lucky we are. A week's suspension and a month of community service. I'd say we got off pretty easy."

For everything Dar "gets," he sure doesn't get this. "That's why you think we're lucky? How about the fact we didn't get killed, falling into that sink hole."

At the landing, Dar raises his good fist. I shake my head, but set my books down. Holding his fist with my left hand, I tap it with my right fist. "It's a bump, Dar. Not a punch!"

When we turn the corner to our hallway, Mack is standing at the door to our classroom. He zeroes in on Dar with his radar eyes and a look like he's going to pounce. "Hey Einstein," he yells, and tries hopping over to us. "How's the wrist?"

Mack's leg is wrapped in a cast and he's using crutches to get around. Dar's arm is in a sling, and me, well with the huge bandage around my head, the three of us look pretty darn cool.

Turns out, everyone at the campground was staring at a huge gash in my scalp. I needed fifty stitches! The drip down my chin and the weird taste in my mouth, well, you get the picture.

Dar says, "My wrist's not so bad. But what's with the leg, Mack? What did you do to yourself? Fall in a hole or something?"

Mack's smile is huge. But before he can answer, we hear it—the sound of clicking heels on the shiny floor.

"Good morning, boys! I hear I wasn't the only one who needed to be rescued." Miss Anders gives Dar and me a hug.

I'm shocked to see her. I figured it'd be months before she'd be back to school. "How'd you get better so soon?"

"You know, Spanky, a little determination goes a long way. I wasn't that bad off. I decided I wanted to be healthy, did everything I was supposed to do, and well, here I am. I owe so much to you and Dar. I haven't forgotten that you two saved my life." She looks at me, then at Dar. "You both, you'll always have a special place in my life."

Mack hobbles over. "Miss Anders, that old thing you just said. About Spanky and Dar. I get it. That whole special place thing. Did you hear Spanky saved my life, too?"

Miss A's smile disappears.

As I watch the two of them stare at each other, I realize I feel the same way about Mack. I guess when you save someone's life or they save yours, you're glued at the hip forever.

"Spanky kept me from freaking out down there in that sinkhole," says Mack. "If I'd have been him, I'd have saved myself. But he didn't. He helped us get through the night."

Miss Anders' forehead wrinkles. She shakes her head as if she doesn't believe a word, and says, "Did I get lost and walk into the wrong school? You sound so different."

Everyone's crowding around. They're talking all at once. To me! Somehow down in that hole, I must have changed from weenie to wonderful.

And speaking of W words, when that worried woman I call Mom came to the hospital, she said she and my dad talked about what Ms. Badu said, about me having garbage on the brain and how I thought I needed to see a shrink. I guess it got her thinking that she's the one who should get some therapy.

So far, not all that much has changed with her, but we're talking more. Plus, some guy at the hospital put us in touch with this group for military families. Seemed kind of lame at first, but then I remembered we used to know Dad's Reserve buddy's families back up north. So we're going to check it out.

Miss Anders walks with us to our classroom. "So, boys, how was your substitute teacher."

Mack, Dar, and I look at each other. After sharing our stories during that long night, we had a few questions for Ms. Badu. But with Miss Anders back, I can tell it's hitting them just like it's hitting me that we won't get to ask them.

Mack smiles at Dar. It's the kind of smile between two guys who are in on a secret no one else knows—no one else but me, that is.

"Guess we'll never really know, Boy Scouts," Mack says, "but I'm pretty sure it was the purple marker."

Miss Anders squinches her eyes, like she's wondering what the heck Mack's talking about. Dar looks as if he's thinking serious thoughts. He rubs his chin. "It's either that or her secret powers." But Dar can't keep the look for long. A smirk sputters into a huge laugh. "If you ask me," he adds, "we were all under her spell. Bwwaaa...Hooo hooo hah hah heee hee."

I raise my fist and Dar bumps it, a little easier this time. "I have no idea what these two bozos are talking about," I say to Miss Anders. "I'm just seriously glad you're back."

Miss Anders was right about the three of us being different. I'd say we became friends, but it was more like blood brothers. Sharing major truths has something to do with it. But so did being scared out of our minds, not to mention losing blood and breaking bones.

I know now I had a few too many things on my mind, what with Dad gone. But talking about them made some space in my brain. It just took me a while to be ready to talk. Maybe that's it. Maybe you just have to be ready.

At the door to our classroom, I hold out my arm to let Dar and Mack by. But a voice coming from a classroom down the hall gets my attention and I know the interesting times at DIP are far from over. It moves through my ears, along my veins, and down to the pit of my stomach.

"Good morrrrning, my children. My name is Ms. Badu. That's baaah like a sheep and do like how doooo you do."

THE END

AUTHOR'S NOTES

I am not in the military. I have never served in the military, nor has my husband nor have my children. The closest I've come to a true connection is my deceased father, Reuben D. Lederman, who flew with the Army Air Force during WWII. But he never shared his difficult memories with me. Still, I overheard them when he talked to his friends—how he became a fatalist, seeing, for example, the mid-air explosion of a plane that had just taken off moments before his. In an odd way, there is a connection between Dad protecting me from the truth to Spanky's ineffective way of coping with his fears by refusing to talk about them.

With no military background, how did I possibly think I could write a story about a boy struggling with the deployment of his dad? I didn't set out to write this story. Spanky began as the story of a boy who wanted to make his dad proud. As a firefighter and a soldier, Dad's persona took on super heroic proportions. As I followed the wars in Iraq and Afghanistan and thought about the number of soldier's serving, two things became apparent. Soldiers are our nation's heroes. So when Spanky considered what he'd need to do to make his super-hero firefighter dad proud, in his mind's eye, his acts would have to be supersized. There is, however, heroism in the everyday acts of sacrifice and survival. So to me, those waiting for a soldier to return—the wives, husbands and children—are heroes as well.

In an interview, I was asked if I had anything to say to military families. I swallowed hard, feeling deeply humbled.

What words could I, a kid's book writer, offer that would have value to a family struggling with deployment? But in a VeteranCentral.com article about Spanky, Twila Camp suggested parents could use Spanky as a way to talk about the difficult issues. That by discussing what Spanky was feeling, children could safely explore their own confusing emotions.

Writing has always been cathartic to me. If I were to suggest anything, perhaps the children who read this might become authors of their own stories.

Spanky endured many years of revision. But I recently received a letter from a soldier who said, "Thank you, because my kids need all the books they can get helping them with my one year deployment to Afghanistan." That one letter made the process worth every minute.

ACKNOWLEDGEMENTS

Under normal circumstances, the Army Reserve does not call up soldiers in the short period of time in which Spanky's dad had been notified. I relied on the technical input from the communications office of the U.S. Army Reserve Command in Seminole, FL who helped me define a plausible reason. An extraordinary author, fellow graduate of Vermont College of Fine Arts and veteran of the Army Reserves, Trent Reedy, provided considerable insight into both the technical and emotional details of deployment. He urged me to write Spanky's story, for the millions of children who navigate life with a parent in the military.

Like all stories, Spanky developed from many influences. In a lecture on the politics of Dr. Seuss, Tobin Anderson inspired my interest in creating subtext that might stimulate children to consider political questions about right and wrong, about war and peace to form their own opinions. I did not intend for the book to provide answers. Instead, I hoped it would help children see that when it comes to war, there are no black and white or easy answers.

Since becoming a kid lit writer in 2004, I have belonged to two Florida critique groups who nurtured Spanky (and me) through many revisions. So you might say Spanky cut his teeth with the love of Augusta Scattergood, Greg Neri, Melissa Buhler, and Teddi Aggeles from one group and Karen Bachman, Madeleine Kuderick, Karleen Tauszik, and last but not least, my angel, Nancy Cavenaugh from the other.

Over many amazing breakfasts, Abe and Marika Spevak, who both read multiple revisions of Spanky, guided me on literary and psychological questions. Their grandson, Noah Antonio Gonzalez, who became my first young critiquer, provided enormously useful insights and recommendations.

I cannot forget growing up with the gang of kids on 14th Street. Their influences helped me flesh out bully, Mack Malone. The greatest influence to my writing life, however, has been the brilliant and wildly successful Vermont College of Fine Arts faculty as well as my equally brilliant and successful S3Q2 family. While studying for an MFA in Writing for Children and Young Adults, these personal heroes helped me dig deeper into craft and realize my worth as a writer.

My life has been blessed. My extraordinary mom, Audrey, generates a river of positive energy and love, my husband and best friend, Don, who believes in me and always gives me space to work, and my children, Sean, Ryan, and Tessa and my daughter-in-laws, Sheila and Nolene, who inspire me with their hard work and success.

Made in the USA
Monee, IL
17 May 2021